Eagles Fly Alone

A Langley Calhoun Mystery

by

Lars R. Trodson

Mainly Murder Press, LLC
PO Box 290586
Wethersfield, CT 06129-0586
www.mainlymurderpress.com

Mainly Murder Press

Copy Editor: Jack Ryan
Executive Editor: Judith K. Ivie
Cover Designer: Mark Dearborn

ISBN 978-0-9836823-0-1

Published in the United States of America

2011

Mainly Murder Press
PO Box 290586
Wethersfield, CT 06129-0586
www.MainlyMurderPress.com

For Judy and Jesse

Acknowledgments

I would like to thank the following people for their invaluable help in preparing this manuscript: James Landis, Rob Ciandella, Debbie Tillar, Rev. Campbell Lovett, Eileen Lovett, Rev. Sid Lovett, Jeanne West, Hannah Lally, Cresta Smith, James Buchanan, Mark Dearborn, and, of course, my parents Don and Pat Trodson.

Book One

One

Saturday, March 27, 7:00 a.m., Fenton, New Hampshire. Langley Calhoun hated death by violence. He had seen three people killed that way, and he truly hated each experience. One was a victim of road rage, another was the body of a young man who had his head split apart by a baseball bat during a pickup game, and the third—this happened when he was a child—was a situation so bad he never liked to talk about it.

A body that has been smashed open is just meat and bone, Langley thought. It is a sad thing because it looks like its mystery and soul have spilled out.

He was seeing these images in his head as he walked behind Antonio Meli, who said he wanted to show Langley a murder victim. Langley, the Chief of Police, knew he wasn't going to see the body of a person. But all the same, because of the cryptic way Antonio had described the situation, he wasn't looking forward to seeing the corpse, whatever it was.

It was warm even for early spring. The earth was wet after the thaw of the long, hard winter. The leaves and the pine needles, the twigs and the loam, had all loosened up into a thick mud. Their shoes sank into the ground and were covered in muck.

Antonio Meli was 82 years old. He was tall and thin—like the top rail of a New England fence, he always said—and his breath was steady. He was one of those Yankees born in the first half of the twentieth century that still trusted the rhythm of the seasons. He wore a light windbreaker, jeans, hiking boots and gloves. Langley was dressed in the casual business style he had adopted when not wearing his uniform, a pressed shirt and slacks. His shoes were all wrong.

They were walking on the back acre of Meli's seven-acre property. This back acre sloped up to the top of a hill and was bordered by a stone wall. On the other side of the wall was a landfill, and Antonio had told Langley earlier that he thought the owners of the landfill were connected to the bit of violence he had found on his property.

Every day for more than a year Antonio had been monitoring that landfill, which was a huge dusty pit that was filled up a bit more each day with the crushed parts of razed buildings. There were piles of bricks and concrete and God knows what else. The material was brought in by trucks that drove up, dumped their load and drove off, over and over, all day, every day except Sunday.

Just a few weeks ago something new happened. There was a flash flood, and a river of sludgy runoff poured down from the high piles of rubble in the landfill and onto Antonio's property.

Antonio took pictures of the hardened pools of sandy concrete, which was flecked with all kinds of debris and garbage, and he contacted the New Hampshire Office of Environmental Protection. Antonio sent repeated letters to the owner of the landfill in an effort to get the company to be a little more respectful, but they were never answered.

Several attorneys had advised him to sue, but Antonio said anything was more palatable than going to court, so he simply pressed on by himself.

As they walked up the hill, Antonio told Langley he suspected the people who ran the landfill were now trying to frighten him. Antonio thought their conventional battle had turned into something more sinister. "They're a bunch of gangsters," Antonio said, "and I mean that literally." He stopped walking and spat out, "Goddamn it."

Langley came up behind him. He looked down and saw the decapitated body of a dead bird.

"Goddamn it," Antonio said again.

"Jesus, Antonio, it's a bird," said Langley.

"That bird has been killed, and someone put it on my property," said Antonio. "Those bastards are trying to send me a message."

Langley knelt down and looked at the animal without touching it. It stank. Its flesh was desiccated. The feathers were matted and broken. The head looked like a dirty, shrunken doll's head. The eyes were dried out but had a trace of fear in them left over from when it had been killed. The slice at the neck was clean, and there was almost no blood on the brown leaves beneath the body. Langley thought it was probably already dead when it had been decapitated.

"Those sons of bitches over there are trying to get cute with me again."

"I heard you," said Langley. He stood. The bird had gray feathers and bright yellow feet and long black talons. There was something strange about it. It didn't look like any bird that Langley had seen before. It looked like an eagle, but an exotic one.

Langley brought out his Blackberry and took pictures of the bird from several angles. He opened a small notebook and made a few notes. "How far are we from your property line," he asked Antonio.

"Maybe ten feet," he said.

"Do you see any other signs of violence? Any other dead or injured animals?"

"No, sir," said Antonio. Langley wrote it down.

"Anything else? Any knives, any kind of weapon, anything at all?"

"No, it was just this."

"How did you happen to come across the bird?"

"I come up here every day to check up on what those bastards are doing," Antonio said with a little more steel in his voice that usual. "You know that, Chief. I'm up here every day, checking my land, checking to make sure that my trees and ground aren't covered in some kind of toxic crap." His voice was raised.

"OK," said Langley. He picked up a stick and inserted the sharp end into the open neck of the bird. He lifted the head and put it in a plastic grocery bag that Antonio had brought along in his back pocket. Langley then jabbed the stick into the open hole of the body. As he brought the body up, Antonio reached over and quickly plucked two feathers off its wings.

Langley then dropped the carcass next to the head in the bag. Something about the sight of the lifeless bird lying in the bottom of a saggy plastic bag filled him with sadness.

"I want you to find out if any of those bastards at that goddamn landfill had anything to do with this," Antonio said, pointing over the stone wall. "They won't scare me."

"They haven't yet," said Langley. "How do you figure this has anything to do with you anyway, or them? It could be just kids."

"Nothing around here ever happens by accident."

Langley looked over the ridge into the landfill. It was relatively quiet for a Saturday morning. But Langley realized that the place had been taking in so much material for the past year that the piles of concrete and brick were now higher than the top of Antonio's hill. Less than a year ago Langley and Antonio had been in the same spot, and they had to look down into the pit. It was still a hole in the ground. But now the landfill, quite literally a hill of refuse, might possibly be the highest peak in all of Fenton.

A truck was unloading its fill. There were four workers on the scene. Two of them had stopped and were looking over at Langley and Antonio. One of them pulled a digital camera out of his pocket, pointed it at Langley and Antonio and took a picture.

"Come on," said Langley, "let's go."

Antonio tied the bag with the bird in it and handed it to Langley. They both walked down the hill and shook hands when they reached Langley's vehicle.

"What are you going to do next?"

"I guess I'll call the Great Bay Reserve and see if they know what kind of bird this is," said Langley.

"That bird is not from around here," said Antonio.

"And then I guess I'll call Bill Plano and ask him if he knows anything about it," said Langley. Bill Plano was the owner of the landfill.

Langley gently put the bag into his passenger seat. He wished he had a more dignified container to put it in. "Be careful," he said to Antonio after he started his car. "They're watching you."

"I'm watching *them,*" said Antonio.

Langley left Antonio's house and hooked onto Goodwin Road to head back to the station. It looked like rain; it felt like rain. It had been raining since early February. The sky was gray and murky, and he recalled conversations he'd had in town with the few farmers that were left. "We need rain," they all said, "but not this much rain."

The *Fenton Herald* had run a headline that said the mosquitoes were going to be bad this summer and the plants would bloom early. But the mosquitoes were already big and fat, and there were blooms on the blueberry bushes. It was only March.

He drove down Goodwin and onto Depot, passing old Carl Deickmann's property. The house had burned down years ago with Carl inside. Langley went by Amsell's Farm. He saw Steve Amsell and a few other guys standing around Steve's old orange Kubota drinking beer. They were laughing about something.

He picked up his phone and pressed the number for Delia Reed, a forest ranger stationed at the Great Bay National Park.

"Great Bay," a voice said.

"Delia? It's Langley Calhoun."

"Langley Calhoun." There was a slight pause. "How are you doing? I haven't heard from you in ages."

"I know. I'm just … how are you?"

"I'm great. What's up?"

"Listen, ah, do you have a minute?"

"I sure do." Delia had a great voice. Langley loved her voice.

"I was called over to Antonio Meli's house this morning. Do you know Antonio?"

"No, sir."

"Well, he called me because he found a dead bird on his property. It was a ... well, it's an eagle. I think it's an eagle."

"You're not sure?"

"Antonio says he's never seen one like it and neither have I."

"OK."

"It was obviously killed." *Murdered* didn't seem like quite the right word, even though that's what Antonio had called it.

"How do you know that?" Delia's voice sounded tense.

"Well, it looks like its head has been deliberately cut off."

"It wasn't in a fight with another animal?"

"The cut looks too clean. It doesn't have any scratches or lesions or anything else."

She let out a deep sigh.

"I have the bird with me, but… Look, if you're there I'd rather show it to you than keep talking about it over the phone."

"Bring it on over," she said and hung up.

Two

Delia Reed was the lone staff member of a federal park that by all accounts should have closed long ago. The congressman representing the district used to hike right where the refuge was located, and he had some fondness for the old trails, so he fought to keep the park and the ranger station open. But every year the budget still got smaller, and the staff dwindled from ten to eight to five to two. Now Delia was the only district ranger left.

Her building itself was sad. It had the look and feel of a convenience store that's no longer stocking its shelves. It was nearly empty and was over-lighted. The park had been carved out of the back end of an old air force base that had been closed more than twenty years ago.

But Delia was always cheerful. She liked being by herself and knew the value of flying low under the radar. Langley was happy to see her. But when he walked in he was suddenly conscious or the dried mud on his dress shoes.

He gently placed the supermarket bag onto the table and untied the handles. Delia brought out a pair of thin rubber gloves and put them on. She handed a pair to Langley. "Have you been handling the animal?" she asked.

"I put both parts into the bag with a stick," said Langley.

Delia lifted the head of the bird out first and then the body. She placed them on newspapers she had spread out.

Then she shook her head. She went over to a counter and took a digital camera off a shelf and started to take pictures of the bird.

"Put it on its belly," she said, and then she snapped some more. "Can you just flip it over? Gently. That's right. Thank you." More photos. "And just lift the wings." Langley did. Then she took one photo of the head and flipped it over herself and took one more shot. Delia put the camera down, stepped back and frowned.

Langley decided just to let her think.

She cocked her head. "That bird is definitely not from around here."

"Was it deliberately killed?"

"I would guess. There's obvious decomposition but no deliberate damage to any other part of the body. It's clean."

"Do you know what it is?"

"It's an eagle, definitely, but ..." She was delicately lifting up the bird's feathers, looking at its face, checking the talons and the markings on its plumage.

"There's no chance it's from around here?" he asked.

"No chance. None."

"What would it be doing around here?"

"This is an animal that somebody brought here illegally and didn't know how to get rid of or sell or whatever it was they were going to do, so they killed it."

"Sell it?"

"If it's rare," Delia said as she took more pictures. "It didn't fly here, I'll tell you that."

Delia took the memory card out of her camera, inserted it into her laptop and uploaded the photos. She arranged them and put them into a folder, then logged on to her email account. She typed in an address and stood up again.

Langley stared at the bird. It couldn't have looked more innocuous or unimportant.

"You said it was on private property?"

"Yeah, but there's a little back story there," Langley said.

"What's that?"

"There's a business, a landfill, right behind Antonio Meli's house, and he's been fighting with them. Now he feels they're sending him a message."

"It sounds a little thuggish," Delia said. "Do you believe it?"

"I don't like the people who own that company any more than the guy does, but it doesn't follow that they would use an, ah, bird to send him a warning. Too obvious. Stupid, really."

"It seems a little crazy."

"I think it was just random," said Langley.

"Not random," Delia sighed. "Somebody brought that bird to your neighborhood. Well," she said, stepping back to look at the bird, "you've got a little mystery on your hands."

"I'll report to Fish & Wildlife and let them deal with it."

"I just sent images to a friend of mine. He'll know what it is right away," she said. "I copied you. We'll find out what it is."

"WHAT DO WE GOT?" SAID ARCH TRIMBLE, PATROL OFFICER FIRST CLASS, when Langley got back to the station.

"What we got," said Langley, "is a dead bird."

"A dead bird? I thought Meli had a corpse."

"He did, only not quite so exciting as a dead person."

"Why did he call you up there?"

"For some reason he thought the bird had been killed unnaturally and, you know, he's a nervous guy. He's an old man. He wants to feel safe."

"Ain't no bird going to hurt Antonio," Arch said. Langley smiled.

"What kind of bird was it," asked Arch.

"I don't know. We're going to find out." Langley put the bag with the bird remains into a freezer.

"Could be trouble," said Arch. Langley felt a bit uneasy when he said that.

Three

Later that afternoon Langley received a text message from Delia Reed. "Crowned solitary eagle. S. America,"it read. "Check ur email."

Then another one came: "Endangered."

"Trouble," said a third, exactly what Arch Trimble had said earlier.

Langley picked up the phone and dialed Delia's number.

"Hey, Chief," she said.

"We got ourselves a little something, huh?"

"Yes, well ..." Delia's voice trailed off.

"What?" asked Langley.

"It just makes me so fucking mad," said Delia. "Report it to Fish & Wildlife, and if there's anything else, just let me know."

"And if you think of anything, let *me* know." Langley didn't want to hang up the phone. He was happy to have this renewed connection with Delia, and he wanted to prolong it, but he had run out of things to say.

"I hope you catch the person who did this," she said.

"Me too," but Langley already had his doubts. They said goodbye. He made a face, a grimace, and looked at the silent phone. He called Antonio.

"Chief," said Antonio when he picked up the phone.

"Hi Antonio, we found out a couple of things about the bird."

"I did, too."

"You did?"

"I just put a description of it into Google, and it came up."

"Well, Christ," said Langley. He was a little annoyed but didn't know why. Maybe he felt a little irrelevant.

"What are we gonna do next?"

"We're gonna turn it over to the Feds," said Langley. "Now, Antonio, don't go around saying anything. Just let it go for now, OK? There are things to figure out, OK? I don't want you to have any contact with Plano or anybody else out there. We'll figure this out soon enough."

On his way home Langley drove by Amsell's Farm. The tractor was still sitting out in the driveway, but Amsell and the rest of the guys were gone. Black bursts of cloud floated against a pale backdrop of dull gray sky. Langley took in a deep breath.

He headed up Depot Road, onto Goodwin, and then to Ambush Rock Road where his little house sat. He pulled in his driveway. Langley's house was dark and as he shut off his car and stared at it.

Langley had bought this place after he and his wife had divorced. Selling their old house was part of their agreement. He always had the vague feeling … hope? ... that it would only be temporary, but he had no plans to go anywhere else. He had lived there now for almost four years.

Tonight the house was bathed in a kind of lavender light. It was not a New Hampshire light. This was the kind of light that descended slowly down onto an ancient desert. The kind of light in which you would see a caravan of nomads driving across the desert on camels, the hooves of the animals sinking in the sand, silently, silently, silently, as the gentle breeze blew the sand and the mute riders stared into the purple distance toward their unknown destination. He pictured the scarves over their faces, their eyes full of intent.

Ah, damn, Langley thought as he got out of the car. He wondered what the people of Fenton would think if they knew their police chief had these silly thoughts. Cops are generally thought to be devoid of poetry and grace. He had a rueful smile and shook his head. If they only knew.

He opened his front door, which he never locked. He hung his keys on a little eye-hook screwed underneath one of the wooden cupboards in the kitchen. He put his phone on the counter. Langley went into his bedroom and took off his holster and put his gun and ID in a small basket on top of his bureau. He took off his shirt and changed into a sweatshirt and went back into his kitchen. He wanted to change out of his shoes and put on a pair of jeans, but he was too tired.

Langley picked out a clean, six-ounce jam jar from the dish rack and placed it on the counter. He poured some red wine into the glass and fizzed it up with some Perrier. He put in an ice cube and took a sip. He switched on the radio. It was set to WSCA, a low-powered community FM station that broadcast out of Portsmouth, which tonight was replaying old radio dramas.

The inside of the house was now a deep blue, and as he listened to the radio he started to fall asleep. He suddenly remembered that Arch was going to send him over some information. He got up and went to his computer.

There were emails from Arch and Delia Reed. There was an email from his ex-wife that he would look at later.

The subject line simply said Papers, and Langley thought he must have been asked to send her something and had forgotten. If she had called instead he could have at least talked to her, but they never spoke any more.

Delia had sent photos of a Crowned Solitary Eagle, which she said could be found in Brazil, Argentina and Bolivia. It was the same bird Antonio had found.

"Long goddamn way from New Hampshire," said Langley out loud.

"There are only two categories for an animal after it's listed as endangered," wrote Delia, "and those are 'extinct in the wild' and 'extinct.' What you have there is a protected animal."

Arch had sent Langley some information on agencies that monitor bird and animal trafficking. Langley made a face. He remembered what Delia had said about someone bringing the bird into the country to sell it.

One of the pictures of the bird showed it perched on a log. There was a chain link fence behind it, so it was obviously in captivity. Langley stared into the bird's face, and he swore it had a forlorn look. He thought the bird looked exactly as though it had thrown a birthday party for itself, and no one had showed up.

Four

Sunday, 7:30 a.m. Langley was shaving while listening to the radio. He listened to a gardening show every Sunday morning, and he was amused at how many times the host recommended using human urine to keep away predatory animals. "Take a cup of human urine," the host recommended, "and pour it around the edge of your garden." Langley smiled.

He shaved slowly, thoughtfully. He brushed his teeth and took a shower and got dressed for church. On the radio the people who called in had moles digging up their lawns and cherry trees that had blight and rhododendrons with brown leaves. He shut off the radio and went to church.

Langley had grown up Catholic, but his family suddenly stopped going to St. Mary's in Kittery when he and his brother Brian were still kids. They were in the car one Sunday morning, and their father simply said, "We're not going to St. Mary's anymore." They started attending Sunday services at the Fenton First Congregationalist Church. At the time Langley had the vague feeling he had switched alliances from one baseball team to another, but it didn't matter. Going to church was an obligation, not something that brought understanding or peace. In any case, it did not bring Langley understanding.

But he kept attending. He was comfortable in these surroundings: the white paint, tall rectangular windows, hardwood pews, columns decorating the facade of the building. Langley and his wife Julia had been married in this church. He remembered the sight of his mother crying in the front row and his father beaming with pride. It had been a boiling hot day in July, and Langley, as nervous as he had ever been in his entire life, draped himself in front of the air conditioner in the minister's office prior to the ceremony and sucked in the frigid, metallic air blowing through the vents.

He liked the pragmatism of the sermons. The minister, Eleanor Kreidel, simply asked the parishioners to do the right thing, and in doing so she employed movie references and elaborate allegories. On this Sunday the congregation heard a story about a catfish. Even though the overall point was obscure, the congregation laughed out loud a couple of times.

Langley was looking at the church program when his brother and his family walked in. He waved gently, and his brother Brian, his wife Eileen and their kids waved back. They were moving to the front of the church. Langley and his brother were no longer angry at each other, not really, but there was a continuation of a lack of closeness that had started years and years ago. The tension that separated them would recede and then resurface at odd times.

Langley thought they were at peace right now, but he also knew that the eagle and Antonio Meli could upset this delicate balance.

Brian Calhoun was the attorney for Bill Plano, who owned the landfill. Brian had been dealing with Meli for years. But Brian had also never really forgiven Langley for opposing the landfill when the company had first decided to locate in Fenton. Brian was the lawyer everyone went to in Fenton if they wanted their land developed or something smoothed out with the code enforcement officer or the zoning boards, and Langley had taken a public stand against his client. He thought Brian and his clients were laying the town to waste.

The two had other issues, but this was one of the thornier ones.

When the service was over, Langley thanked the pastor at the front door as she greeted the parishioners. He shook her hand, and he waited for Brian and his family under the elm tree in the front yard of the church. The sky was blue, and the breeze was gentle. There was pollen in the air. During the hour they were inside the church, each car was covered with a light dusting of the yellow powder.

Langley looked up at the sky and took a note to remember for as long as he could just how beautiful the day was. His reverie was broken by the tight, low hug of his niece Emily, who at eight years old had a sharp wit. Emily had started to call Langley Bigs, as in Big Man. When she hugged him, she said, "Uncle Bigs!" They had long talks together because they were kindred spirits, and Langley thought she was lovely and frail. Danny, his nephew, loped over and offered his hand in an adult way. He was ten. Danny looked exactly like his father and grandfather. Langley hugged his brother's wife Eileen, and then he hugged his brother.

"That was quite a service," said Brian with a cigarette between two fingers. "What was the deal with the catfish?"

"Something about following your true path, I think," said Langley. "Make up your mind what you want to be."

"You mean either a fish or a cat," said Brian. "Well, she's convinced me."

"Do you want to come over and eat?" Eileen asked.

"Yes, yes, come on, Bigs," said Emily, who tugged at Langley's hand.

"That would be great," Langley said, looking down at Emily, who smiled back. He looked at Eileen, who also smiled, and he knew she wondered why he was always by himself, why he never brought anyone over.

"What's going on in town, anything I should know about?" Brian asked.

"Well, yeah, actually. Antonio Meli called me ..."

"Oh, Christ," said Brian.

"Just hold on a second. Tony said he had a dead body on his property."

"Kids," said Eileen quickly. Emily and Danny had suddenly stopped playing and looked up.

"No, no, it turned out to be a bird, a dead bird."

"That isn't funny," said Eileen. "You don't have to be so dramatic about it."

"It turns out this was a rare bird, a South American eagle."

"Strange," said Brian.

Eileen started to herd the kids over to the car. When they were out of earshot, Langley said the bird had been killed deliberately and that he had brought it over to the wildlife reserve.

"Who knows about this?" asked Brian.

"Me, Tony, the ranger at the reserve ..."

Both Brian and Langley said at exactly the same time, "and whoever did it."

Brian squeezed the coal of his cigarette out onto the lawn and then put the filter in his pocket.

"How did it get here?" Brian was looking at his kids when he asked the question.

"I don't have any idea. Antonio thinks ..."

"I know what Antonio thinks," said Brian.

"Well, at any rate, I'm going to call Bill Plano tomorrow and just try to ..."

"I'll call," said Brian, "not you. Where was the bird found?"

"It was way out back near the landfill on top of the hill near the stone wall."

"I don't know what to tell you," said Brian.

THE CALHOUN HOUSE SMELLED OF HAM AND SWEET POTATOES. Langley sat in his chair with a Budweiser. He liked being around his family because their mother and father had never in all their lives talked down to their children or excluded them from any conversation. When they were growing up, they always seemed like a team. Langley and his brother always had a feeling of, well, not quite importance but respect. They talked to each other then. They had to, in a way. And so, despite the trouble, he liked being around his family. Langley wanted to rekindle that camaraderie, but neither he nor Brian really knew how to do that.

Eileen was an excellent cook, and her desserts always looked like they came out of a Martha Stewart magazine. She had made some sort of upside down pineapple cake with thick dark sugar crusting the fruit on the top of the cake.

"That was unbelievable," said Langley as he put down his spoon.

"Do you want to play some cards, Bigs?" Emily liked to play poker. Langley put down his napkin and said, "Sure."

"Emily, give your uncle a minute to relax," said Eileen.

"No, no," said Langley. "It's OK." Danny had gone off to play by himself, which reminded Langley of himself and Brian when they were growing up, always off on their own. Just as he got up from the table someone's phone rang. It was their father, who lived on the other side of town.

Timothy Calhoun had had a heart attack the previous October. He was home now, recuperating. Brian and Langley didn't, in fact, know just how bad their father had looked before the heart attack until they saw how he looked now. Ten months ago he was gray and sallow. Today his cheeks were pink, and he had energy. Timothy Calhoun was sixty-eight years old, and he was such a fatalist that he was convinced he was dying even though the doctors vigorously told him he wasn't. He had been lucky, though. One day when he was out hunting, his right arm felt squeezed and his jaw ached, so he drove himself to the hospital despite having had more beers than he could count. He was drunk, but he had saved his own life.

"The doctor said ..." Eileen was saying into the phone, but she was being interrupted by the cranky old man. "Here," she said with exasperation when handing the phone to Brian. "Your father is dying, and there is apparently nothing that can be done about it."

Brian took the phone. "What's up, Dad?" He listened. "Dad, you just had a new stent put in. They worked like hell on your jaw. It's going to hurt. There's nothing ..." He paused. "Well, if you're life is winding down, then it's winding down." Brian looked at Langley and rolled his eyes and smiled.

Langley knew the old man was suffering now as only a man who had enjoyed good health his entire life could suffer. He served one tour in Vietnam and didn't get so much as a bruise. This was something he boasted about over the years, but later he said he felt ashamed about it. He felt guilty. But as guilty as he felt about some things in his life, he was never sick, had never even been in the hospital. Not until he had that heart attack, which he still seemed unable to account for.

Brian looked at Langley, silently asking if he wanted to talk to his father. Langley thought for a moment and shook his head no. "Tell him I'll call him this week," he said, but Brian didn't pass along the message.

"OK, old man. Goodbye. You were a pretty good dad, when all was said and done." Brian was laughing, but obviously his father on the other end of the line didn't appreciate the joke. "Oh, I'm just kidding, Dad. No, listen, take your nitro, and if you feel any pain call 9-1-1. Got it? Immediately. OK. Do you need to talk to anyone else? One last time? No? OK, Dad, bye. We love you."

LATER, LANGLEY SAT ALONE IN HIS LITTLE HOUSE WITH A JAR of wine in his hand and thought about Delia Reed. He had been looking for a reason to call her for months and months, and if she actually knew how much she was on his mind ... well.

He called his home The Postwar Villa because one day a few years ago, when he had offered to take Delia home from some event, he drove by his house with her in the car. He pointed it out and she said, "Oh, it's a little postwar villa." And so, ever since, he called it his Postwar Villa.

The CD he was listening to ended, and he just sat in the chair and listened to the crickets.

His day was ending on a quiet note, but the next one began loud and white hot.

Five

Monday. On the front page of *The Fenton Herald* there was a picture of an unhappy Antonio Meli standing at the spot where the eagle had been found. The story had quotes from Meli and Delia Reed as well as a sentence that read, "Fenton Police Chief Langley Calhoun did not return repeated messages by press time."

Langley looked at his phone. He had dozens of messages. His Monday morning routine was going to be disrupted, but it was always disrupted. He liked to go to Ruggerio's Market, which was owned by the family of one of the cops on the Fenton force, and buy copies of *The Fenton Herald* and *The New York Times.*

They had a little coffee shop in Ruggerio's, and every morning he ordered his coffee, black, and bought an egg and bacon sandwich on an English muffin. He always wanted to eat the sandwich and drink the coffee in peace while reading the papers and then head into the station. But that never, ever happened. This routine was the very definition of insanity. He did it every day looking for a different result.

Someone inevitably walked up to offer a complaint or ask a question, and today the person whose job it was to do that was Maria Tull. She was not only Langley's dentist, but she was also the chairman of the Fenton Board of Selectmen. She was not the chairwoman, mind you, or the chairperson, she was the Chairman. Langley called her The Little One because she stood just about five feet tall, but never to her face.

"How are you certain that Meli didn't put that bird there himself?" she said.

"And good morning to you, too."

"I'm talking to you as an elected official."

Langley folded up his newspaper.

"Meli's trying to do something funny with A & J Fill & Gravel," Maria said, stating the full name of the company that owned the landfill behind Meli's house.

"What would one have to do with the other?" asked Langley. "Antonio thinks that the landfill folks are trying to pin something on *him*."

"Why in the world would you think that?"

"I don't think that, Maria, I'm just ..."

"That's a good taxpaying citizen." She was talking about the landfill company. Everybody always talked about how much money that company brought into the town because it was virtually the only industry Fenton had. Years ago there were leather tanning companies all along the Oquossoc River, but the last one had closed thirty years ago, and then the town was all but forgotten.

"Maria, Madame Chairwoman ..."

"Don't be funny," she said as she moved right up to Langley's face.

"I'm going to find out who did it," said Langley.

"I want you to put a leash on Meli," she said.

"How can I do that?"

"No one cares about his problems with that stupid bird."

"Well, first off, the feds may care."

"The Feds?"

"Fish & Wildlife, Maria, because this is apparently a rare animal."

"Animal? It's a bird."

"I know that, but now that it's in the paper, I'm sure we'll attract the attention of some other people."

"Who?"

"PETA and the Audubon Society or ..."

"I said don't try to be funny. And by the way, I think the Chief of Police should respond when a reporter calls," said Maria.

Just then Langley's phone rang. It was Delia. He pushed "ignore." His phone rang a second time, and it was his brother. The third time it rang it was Antonio Meli. Then *The Fenton Herald* called. Then there was a call from an agent from U.S. Fish & Wildlife.

As Langley looked at the calls, Maria huffed.

"Maria, I have to return these calls."

"Now he answers the phone," she said. "I'm going to put you on next week's agenda so you can update the town about this." She began to walk away. "I don't want any trouble about that bird."

Langley got on the phone with a Fish & Wildlife biologist. He told the agent, Martin Poll, that he would forward the photographs he had of the bird. The agent asked if he had destroyed the bird. Langley said it was in a freezer at the police station.

"If you have an update, please let me know," said Martin.

Langley then called his brother back. "It would behoove you to come over here and talk to Mr. Plano and let him know that you are not focusing on A&J in your investigation of who killed this bird." Behoove was Brian's favorite word. Bill Plano was the president and CEO of A&J Fill & Gravel.

Langley actually chuckled, "Well, investigation is, ah, a funny word, Brian, because I was told about the thing just yesterday."

"I'm just saying."

"You want me to come over and talk to Plano?"

"His company is in the paper, being accused ..."

"The company was not accused of anything."

"And your friend Meli, did you tell him to go to the paper?"

Langley wanted to tell his brother to fuck off. "I didn't tell Antonio anything. It never even occurred to me to go to the media. I was busy trying to figure out what the thing was and why the hell it was even here. I told you that at church."

"Plano's phone is blowing up, so I think it would be a good idea to come over here and reassure him."

"About what, exactly?" Langley sighed.

"How about a courtesy call, *Chief*," said Brian. "Let him know where you're at."

"Are you planning on being there if I come over?"

"Of course."

Langley sighed.

"Be here at two."

"OK." And then suddenly Langley said, "You come to my office, actually. One-thirty."

LANGLEY TOOK A DRIVE OVER TO THE FENTON HERALD AND with a copy of the morning paper in his hand walked up to the reception desk and asked for Les Miller, the executive editor. The two men knew each other pretty well. When he walked into Les's office, there was a young woman sitting in one of the two chairs. He assumed it was the reporter who had written the story about the bird.

"This is Britney Sawuko," said Miller, and Langley shook her hand.

"Hi," she said, standing to shake Langley's hand. Langley hadn't met her before, but he could tell she was smart and confident.

"We called you, Chief. Britney says she called you three times last night," said Miller.

Langley opened his phone and read out the number that had called him repeatedly the night before. "Is that your number?" he asked Britney and she said it was. "Then she called. My fault. I'm not here to complain. I think you might have done me a favor." He turned to the reporter. "Can I ask if it was Mr. Meli that called you about the bird?"

"He called me yesterday," she said. "He didn't tell me anything that was off the record."

Langley didn't know if he was relieved or frustrated that it was Antonio that called. If it had been someone else, it could have led somewhere.

Britney Sawuko flipped open her notebook and clicked her pen. "Can you tell us what's going on?"

"We took the decapitated bird, its head and body, over to the Great Bay Reserve at Newington to try to get a better idea of whether the bird was killed deliberately or if it was a natural death."

"We know all that, Chief. It's in the paper," said Miller.

"Does the bird have any significant value, monetary value?" asked Britney.

"I have no idea."

"Have you done a blood screen on it or anything like that," she asked.

"I hadn't even thought of that," said Langley, "but I think I will now. That's off the record." He looked at the two of them. "I guess what I want is that for whoever is out there pulling this shit to know that we're going to stay on it. So I want you to stay on it."

"Can you say that on the record?" asked Britney.

"I plan on being vigorous and thorough in my investigation of this incident," he said. "Fenton is a community that respects nature, and this act is contrary to our beliefs." Langley was using his on-the-record voice. "If there is anyone who knows anything about this crime or who brought the bird into Fenton, then we encourage them to come forward."

Britney was writing this down. "What else?"

"I've contacted the U.S. Fish & Wildlife Department. There are federal laws protecting these animals, so they're now involved, too," Langley said. "I have one more thing," he added, indicating he was speaking on the record. "It's important to know that neither I, nor the Fenton P.D., nor any other local government official, is aligned with any comments that may have been made by private citizens about this matter. They're entitled to their opinions, but we will go about this investigation with an open mind and without prejudging anyone or anything."

"Plano up your ass?" Les Miller asked.

"First thing this morning," said Langley.

"That asshole," said Miller. "I heard he was going to run for Selectman. Oh, Christ, why can't these people just leave us alone?"

"So this bird is definitely endangered?" asked Britney.

"This is an endangered species of bird," said Langley. "Definitely classified that way. You can verify that."

Deb Schoff, the paper's photographer, walked into the office with her camera around her neck.

"Deb, I want you and Britney to go over to the Great Bay Reserve," Miller said. "Just hang around there for a little while to see if there is anything going on."

It was just then that Langley remembered that he needed to call Delia back.

ON HIS WAY OUT OF THE NEWSPAPER'S PARKING LOT, DELIA called again. "The media are here," she said.

"What media?"

"There's got to be five or six dish trucks out front. Reporters from Boston, FOX, Channel 9, and a few print reporters. My inbox is full of media requests." She sounded distraught.

"OK, OK. It'll be all right. Have you talked to anyone yet?"

"I had to call Russell's office. I'm not allowed to talk to the media after the story today. I've apparently violated guidelines." She sighed. "Someone from Russell's office is coming over." Gene Russell was the congressman who represented the district.

"OK," Langley said. "We'll be there in just a few minutes." He then pushed Britney Sawuko's number.

"This is Britney Sawuko," she said when she picked up the phone.

"It's Chief Calhoun, Britney. I hate to tell you, but you don't have this story all to yourself any more. There are media reps at the Reserve from all over."

"Oh, shit," she said.

"Good luck," said Langley.

He called Antonio. "Antonio, I asked you not to say anything. I specifically asked you not to say anything to anybody about this. Now we have a real mess, you know."

"Chief, I only took it as a suggestion, and at any rate I have no interest in letting Plano or anybody else think they're getting away with shit," he said.

"I get it, Antonio, but I wanted to be able to control this story maybe a little bit," Langley said.

"We're gonna smoke those bastards out," said Antonio.

"I gotta go," said Langley. He parked his vehicle in the ranger station parking lot. There were a few hikers and walkers looking at the scene. As soon as Langley stepped out of the car, the reporters were upon him. He continued to verify the established facts: where the bird had been found, by whom, what kind of bird it was. Where they thought it was from. No one knew how it got to Fenton or who had killed it. He stuck to the facts.

Langley knew why the media people were there. It wasn't just the bird. The media loved the idea of crusty old Antonio Meli going up against the local business. Yankee Individualism, the headlines would scream. How the media loved a cliché.

The staff member from Congressman Russell's office that had come to Fenton to deal with the media was a tall, inordinately thin, blond young man in a nice suit. His job was apparently to repeat the same statement all day long: "No one appreciates the beauty of nature more than Congressman Russell. He is a leader in protecting our natural resources in Congress. Congressman Russell, with the support of federal and local officials, is determined to find who is behind this terrible crime."

"I didn't know there were any natural resources in Congress," Langley said to Delia after the staffer had left.

"Ssshhhhh," said Delia, laughing. "Don't say that. The guy funds my little office here. Don't make fun."

At one-thirty Langley was sitting in his office waiting for his brother Brian and Bill Plano. He was wondering whether he should have put on his tie. Just for show he put his badge on his desk, and he made sure his gun was properly holstered. It was a stupid, juvenile display of authority, but his brother always made Langley feel so small.

By two-fifteen Langley was simply pissed. By two-twenty-five he was ready to leave the office for the day and to tell his brother and his precious client to go to hell. They never showed.

When Langley watched the stories later that night, he was happy to have held his ground. In his quotes he kept focused on the bird. And there was Bill Plano, accusing Antonio Meli of slander and accusing the Fenton Police Department—that would be Chief Langley Calhoun—of not having much control over the town.

Six

Tuesday. Langley's alarm clock beeped at six a.m. The sky was pale blue, the birds were chirping, and the trees just outside Langley's window were almost in full bloom.

Maple syrup season had come and gone in a flash. The local sap harvest was about a third of its normal output. Early spring had been too warm and wet, and the thaw came too early. As he looked at the leaves on the trees, Langley vaguely wondered if the leaves weren't going to turn while it was still summer. They had leafed out a month early, so maybe they would turn early, too. He worried because maybe the tourists wouldn't come. Every year busloads of tourists came through the town to look at the leaves, and it was good for the local economy. Maybe this would be the year that nature finally rebelled.

After he showered, shaved, brushed and dressed, his phone rang and he said hello to his father.

"You looked mighty fine on the TV last night there, son."

"Thanks, Dad."

"Very proper."

"I'm sure."

"They spelled your name wrong."

"Just on one of the stations." Langley's father often pointed out that the original spelling of their name was Colquhoun, which was the name of Langley's grandfather, who had anglicized it when he came to America in the 1920s.

"What are you doing for breakfast?" asked his father.

"I was going to go out and meet my public."

"I'll be your bodyguard. No paparazzi! No paparazzi!" His father's imitation of an Italian accent was terrible.

"Sure, old man. Where do you want to meet?"

"Just come over to the house. I have something to tell you."

Next to the driveway of the house that Langley grew up in was the most spectacular maple tree in town. It had an enormous trunk and a huge, perfectly shaped canopy. The limbs lifted gracefully to the sky, and ever since he was a kid Langley had been comforted by the sound of the breeze as it rustled its leaves.

When he pulled into the driveway, his father was sitting in the wooden swing that he had tied to one of the big lower limbs more than forty years ago. He was drinking a cup of coffee, and he had a traveling cup on the ground waiting for Langley.

The maple leaves rustled gently, and Langley was happy to hear that sound and to see his father. It was a lovely tableau, and Langley walked over and hugged his old man.

He handed Langley the cup of black coffee. "How do you suppose you're going to catch the perp who killed that bird?" the old man asked.

"I don't know," said Langley. "Luck, maybe."

"It seems odd someone would go on private property to do something like that."

"I thought about that, but Antonio's property has a conservation easement on one side and is bordered by the landfill along the back end, so there's a lot of room out there. It's quiet."

"So," said the old man. "Julia called last night."

"What did she want?"

"She wanted me to come down and see the kids."

"Are you feeling up to it?"

"I don't think she meant tomorrow, but it's been a while since I've seen my grandchildren."

"You ought to go."

"I am going to go. I'm not asking permission. I'm just letting you know."

Langley's ex-wife Julia was married to a cop in Allentown, Pennsylvania. She was happy. Their two kids, two girls, were living in a big, happy, blended family. They dutifully called Langley on the phone and wasted no time in hanging up.

There was no rationale to his resentment. It was just good old-fashioned jealousy, but it was also a feeling that never went away. Langley had the perpetual sensation of being in high school, of being the kid always on the outs with everyone, of being jealous of every girl in class because they always liked somebody else.

He hated the way these thoughts made him feel. Julia had reinforced those feelings when she left. She had said that he was mentally cruel, and he knew what she meant. He hated the sound of those words, because he did not think of himself as a cruel person, not in any sense. But what she called cruel was Langley's inability to be present, as their kids would say. *Dad, you're just not present.* Julia would sit in a chair, and he wouldn't realize that she had been staring at him for fifteen or twenty minutes. She would simply say, "Where are you?" He was the "nowhere man."

Julia believed he was unhappy and constantly thinking of ways to escape, but that wasn't it at all. Langley was simply trying to figure out the world in which he lived. His own time was vaguely threatening to him. It seemed unknowable. It was why he was fixated on old movies, old photographs, old records. He looked at these things as a kind of door. If he surrounded himself with these antique things, he could walk through them to the settled past. That world was done, Langley said to himself. There were no surprises. People know how their lives turned out. The world in which he lived now was full of surprises, and Langley didn't like that.

And so his wife had had enough. "I can't take it anymore," she said, and there was no sadness in the eyes of their children, because they had had enough, too.

"Son?" His father had been repeating his name.

"Oh, I don't know, Dad."

"I lost you for a second there."

"I sometimes, you know, miss the kids."

"Only sometimes?"

"I can't be unhappy all the time." Langley was looking at the old tree.

"If anyone can be unhappy all the time, you can."

Langley sighed. "Is that what you wanted to talk about? Julia?"

"No, no. I want to tell you that I'm going on a date."

Langley's eyes opened. He smiled. "Well, good for you, old man."

"She's a young woman by my standards,"

"Oh, my God, she'll be caring for you twenty-four hours a day."

"She's a big, chesty girl. Absolutely delicious."

"Jesus, Dad."

"Well, I'm just saying."

"Remember to bring your nitro if she's going to get you all fired up." Langley paused. "Should you be fooling around so soon after your heart attack?"

"I was told to get out, live life."

"What's her name?"

"Vance."

"Vance?"

"Vance. You know something else?"

"No, I do not."

"She's black."

Langley smiled. "Well, Daddy-o, you have yourself a rockin' good time." Langley looked at his father, who was pushing himself around with his feet in the old swing. The old man had a big, friendly grin on his face.

"You look happy," Langley said. It was a thought he meant to keep to himself, but it just came out.

"I am happy."

"Mom would be happy."

"Oh, your mom's all right." Langley's mother had died more than six years ago.

"I'll see you, Dad." Langley turned to go to his car. "Let me know how you make out on that date."

Langley's father waved, and he drank the rest of the coffee that was in Langley's cup.

Seven

Wednesday. Arch Trimble told Langley that his brother was in his office.

"He's a day late," Langley said. "What's that you've got there?" Arch had a report in his hand.

"We've got an DUI downstairs from last night," he said.

"Who is it? Local?"

Arch handed the report to Langley.

"Nicole Noel." Langley read. "Point two-five. She was hammered."

"Do you know her?"

"No," said Langley. "I guess I'm still surprised when we pick up a girl for that. Drinking and driving used to be such a guy thing."

"She's nineteen," said Arch.

"Well," said Langley, "she's going to have a hard road. How did she behave?"

"Tommy Renahan handled it."

"Why's she still here?"

"She was a little wild. Car's impounded."

"OK," said Langley. "Have her clean up. Let her go."

He continued to stare at her file. Langley knew what would happen to that young girl. She'd lose her license but keep driving so that she wouldn't be fired from her job. Public transportation in New Hampshire is practically nonexistent, so if you don't have a car, you're out of luck.

But soon she'd get arrested again, probably for another DUI or for driving without a license or both. She would then lose her license for a year or maybe longer. She would be forced to take a useless DUI course that she couldn't afford. Then she'd lose her job because there would be no way to get to work. She would wind up on assistance and become a regular in the criminal justice system. It was as simple as that. Langley sighed. He handed the file back to Arch. He got up and walked into his office.

Brian was looking out Langley's window, which had a view of the parking lot. He turned around when he heard Langley come in. Langley nodded to his brother. "Brian."

"Chief," he said blankly.

"You're about twenty hours late."

"We had a little PR issue yesterday," said Brian, "thanks to you."

"You still should have called. And I had nothing to do with it. I thought Plano wanted to speak to me, too."

"I'll have to do for now."

Langley wanted to ask Brian if he was Plano's errand boy, but he let it go.

"Meli's accusation ..." Brian said.

"Antonio Meli did not accuse anybody of anything. Jesus, Brian, we talked."

"His query to the media about whether A & J had anything to do with a fuckin' dead bird made their phones ring off the hook," said Brian.

"That's a civil issue."

"It may very well be. Look, I'm not here to fight with you."

"I was unaware we had anything to fight about," said Langley.

"I had people from the fuckin' federal government call me yesterday, asking questions, asking if there were surveillance tapes. I'm sorry if I did not have time for the mighty fuckin' Fenton P.D."

"Jesus, Brian, you're talking like Bill Plano," said Langley.

Brian looked like he was going to spit on Langley's floor. His face was red.

"Do you have any surveillance tapes?" Langley asked.

Brian held up his hand. "Bill's got an offer," he said. "He's gonna put up a fifteen-hundred-dollar reward to anyone that provides information leading directly to the arrest of someone connected to the death of that eagle."

"That may actually help," said Langley.

"That's why he's doing it. To actually help," said Brian in a brutally condescending tone. "All we'd like for you to do is hold a little press conference with Bill to affirm our commitment to finding the perpetrator and to announce the offer of the reward."

"That's it?" But Langley was being sarcastic. "You saw what I said in the paper today. I think that was clear."

"And we appreciate that, but we also would like you to do this," said Brian.

"Brian ..."

"Your position on the landfill is not exactly neutral," said Brian.

"What does that have to do with anything? And anyway that was a long time ago," said Langley. "I don't have a position anymore."

"What it has to do with is if you hadn't sided so closely with those who opposed that business, then people like Antonio Meli wouldn't say stupid things in public," said

Brian. "They think they have cover from you."

"So sue him. He has no cover from me."

"They're emboldened by you," said Brian. His voice was rising. Langley knew and Brian knew that they could be heard outside the office. Brian wanted to be heard. He wanted people to hear him berate his younger brother.

"Keep your goddamn voice down," said Langley.

"I will not keep my voice down, *Chief*," Brian said. "Plano is making a serious offer here. This incident has brought unwanted attention to the town, to your police force."

"What?"

"We want to turn this thing around as best we can. This is a legitimate offer to law enforcement, and you should take it."

"I haven't said I wouldn't. I just may not want … "

"Langley, if it was a local animal shelter or the Congregational Church making an offer, you'd take it in a second," said Brian. "Would you hesitate to hold a press conference with those assholes?" Jesus, Langley wanted to tell his brother to shut up.

"No," he said right away. He was being truthful, but he was also white hot.

"Why don't we do this thing tomorrow, while this story is still national?" said Brian.

"I'll have to think about it," said Langley.

"Public relations will call the media. We'll have something set up in front of the office at A & J Gravel for tomorrow morning. We want to be on the news by noon," said Brian. "Be there or not, but if you are not there, Bill will say that you were invited and didn't show."

After Brian left the office, Langley sat in his chair and

looked out the window. He watched as Brian walked back to the Mercedes waiting in the parking lot. A passenger side window rolled down to reveal Bill Plano sitting in the car. Plano was being emphatic about something. Brian listened, spoke for a second, and when Plano responded, Brian laughed. Langley could tell that it was Brian's fake, sycophantic laugh.

Langley felt disgusted by the two of them. He was disgusted by a guy like Bill Plano, who had become so self-absorbed he no longer cared whether anyone really laughed at his jokes or not.

And he was disgusted by his brother, who was a talented, successful guy, a guy who had a loving family and a wide circle of friends, but who somehow had put himself in the position of having to laugh at unfunny jokes in order to keep earning money from a ridiculous man.

Eight

It was early evening, and the air was warm and languid. Delia Reed looked up and seemed genuinely happy to see Langley walk through the door of the ranger station.

"Hey," she said. Delia was sitting on the floor, cross-legged, putting together a new mini storage unit. The plans were spread out before her, and she had a screwdriver in her hand and a bottle of Heineken at her knee.

"How's it going?" Langley asked.

"Well, we're trying to get this place back in shape. I'll tell you one thing, people have been calling Russell's office to let him know how much they love this place, so actually kind of a good thing happened with all the press. We're sprucing it up a little bit."

"Well, something positive."

"You want a beer? Are you off duty?"

"Sure."

"Sure, you're off duty or sure, you want a beer?"

"Both."

"Good."

Delia uncrossed her legs and stood straight up without using her hands to brace herself. Langley gave her a look, and she said, "Yoga." She pulled a green bottle out of a paper bag, pried the cap off with a bottle opener and handed it to him.

"Thanks."

"Drink up. You've had a helluva couple of days. How are you?"

"Oh," was all he said with a shrug of the shoulders.

"I bet," Delia said. Her voice and face were smiling.

"Listen, who would we go to have an autopsy done on the bird?"

"An autopsy? Why would you do an autopsy?"

"I figure we might want to make sure we've covered all the angles. See if there was any other, um, you know, to find out if the bird was poisoned or ..."

"That seems kind of redundant. Poison the bird and then chop off its head."

"Someone had suggested it."

"You don't want an autopsy. You want a blood test," said Delia.

"That's what I meant, right." Being around Delia always made him self-conscious, and he fumbled things.

"Take it to the state pathology lab, have them draw some blood," she said, then thought for a second. "I don't know if freezing it would have an effect on any toxins present. It might. I just don't know."

They drank their beer and talked a little bit more about how she felt as though there might be a brighter future for her little reserve. She said she had been pessimistic for the past year. She talked and talked, and Langley didn't interrupt. He just looked at her, sitting down on the floor, fiddling with the Phillips head screwdriver, and he listened and listened.

Langley thought this was the perfect moment to ask her out on a date. He thought certainly she would say yes, but he didn't ask. He just shook his head when he tried to figure out the source of his reluctance. He didn't know what held him back.

Nine

Langley was going over his budget. He was looking at Fenton, as he did every time this year, as a series of statistics and dollars.

Fenton, New Hampshire, is fifteen square miles in size, almost to the foot. It's wedged into the easternmost tip of the state. Fenton is bordered by the mighty Piscataqua River on one side and a much smaller river, the Oquossoc, runs north to south through the town, almost splitting it in half.

The last census recorded Fenton's population at six thousand, three hundred ninety-nine, with women slightly outnumbering men. This has not led to any kind of unprecedented population growth. The median income is $52,606. The estimated median house or condo value is $288,722, due mostly to all the waterfront land. The town was created in 1640 and chartered in 1863 and was originally called Oquossoc, but that old Indian word was replaced in the early nineteenth century with Fenton, which was the name of one of the prominent families in town at the time.

Today, there is a Fenton Road and a Fenton Lane; there is a Fenton Lake and a Fenton Point. The local cemetery, notable for its iron archway over the entrance, is filled with Fentons. They were mill owners and politicians and writers, and there was always a vague aura of disrepute hovering over all of them.

The town is run by a five-member board of selectmen. The chairman, chosen by receiving the most votes in the general election, is the top office holder. That's Maria Tull, who does a lot of *pro bono* dentistry work for residents, coincidentally enough. There is no mayor, but there is a town manager, a treasurer, a town clerk with a two-person staff, and a highway department of five.

The tax rate is $14.08 per thousand, and tax bills are sent out in November and June. The town has an operating budget of $26.7 million, with about $14 million going to the school department and another $3.3 million earmarked for the police department. The budget committee has seven members, but one position on that board is vacant. With the even number of people, there have been a few tie votes, but no one seems to volunteer for the position.

The Fenton Police Department has eleven active employees. It has a total of fourteen positions, but two of them are unfilled because of budget shortfalls and one because of a scandal.

Langley Calhoun has been Chief for eight years. *Eight years of ambiguous feelings about the job,* he thought. But now, this year, he was not so much anxious as pensive. He could feel the rumble beneath his feet coming from the people who were going to try to put him out of a job.

He had started out as a patrolman in nearby Berwick, Maine. He did that for three years and came back to Fenton. Now he has one lieutenant, Bill Rogers; one vacant sergeant's position; two detectives; one patrolman first class, Arch Trimble; three officers; a community resource officer; one vacant patrolman's position; a volunteer chaplain; and a harbor master.

Langley laughed when he thought of his harbor master, currently on unpaid leave after having been indicted for taking bribes by allegedly selling buoys in the harbor, much sought after by the newly rich, to the highest bidder. Buoys are usually awarded through a lottery system, but this guy thought of a new way of handing them out. Langley had taken some heat for that. He was accused of not being able to keep his own department in control. What no one knew was that Langley had been working quietly with the Fish & Game Department and the state Attorney General's office to help secure the indictments.

Anyway, that's what the town looks like, on paper. In life, though, a place like Fenton is always buzzing. Of course, what people were buzzing on now was the eagle.

Rumors were flying. On the blog that covered town gossip, fentonville.com, the conversation was particularly uninhibited. Langley read it faithfully every night. There were theories that he was covering up for the bird flu … that he was covering up for A&J Fill & Gravel because his brother is their attorney, if you didn't know … that he was covering up for some cult activity in town … and that they were investigating illegal animal trafficking. The last one at least seemed like it could be true.

There were more than a few comments from people saying that Langley was a drunk.

That stung.

Langley was scrolling down the page to look for more comments about himself—he knew this was no good for him, but he did it anyway—when his doorbell rang. He looked at his watch and wondered who it could be.

It was Maria Tull and Orly Bigelow. Orly was also on the Board of Selectmen. They each nodded their hellos. Orly took off his hat. Maria got to the point.

"Our understanding, Chief, is that Bill Plano is giving a press conference tomorrow morning offering a reward for the bird, and you're not supporting this measure."

Langley wanted to correct her. He wanted to say that Plano isn't offering a reward for the bird, you dolt, but for the capture of whoever killed the bird.

"That isn't true at all. I am supporting the reward. I told him it would be very helpful."

"It seems to us," said Orly, twisting his hat in his hands, "that it would be very simple for you to go over there in the morning and support this thing to keep everything on an even keel."

Langley had a specific and visceral dislike for the phrase "on an even keel" because it was another one that his brother used all the time. On occasion Brian would even say, "It would behoove you to keep this thing on an even keel."

Maria jumped in. "Chief, A & J Fill & Gravel is the largest taxpaying business in this town."

"I know that, Chairman."

"They single-handedly donated five hundred thousand dollars to the upkeep of the high school pool last year, do you remember that?"

"Yes, I do."

"It's important for everyone, not just for people who have kids in the schools, you know," Maria said. Orly Bigelow made a face. Even he thought that was too much.

Langley winced. His kids once were in the schools and had swimming meets in that pool. Maria Tull knew that.

"Maria, I didn't say I wouldn't go, but it was a little difficult because they were more or less ordering me to do it."

"Do you know who you work for, Chief?"

"Of course I do," but Langley knew Maria was going to say it out loud anyway.

"The taxpayers," she said.

"Right."

"We just want to put this whole unpleasant thing behind us, don't you agree?"

"I certainly do," Langley said.

"Go to the press conference, Chief, and make everybody happy," said Maria Tull. She paused and looked at him. "Are you OK?"

"I'm fine," he said.

"You look tired."

"I'm OK. Thanks for asking." And he meant it. He thought she was asking as his dentist, as a doctor.

"You need to be up to this task, Chief."

Then Langley realized she wasn't asking about his well-being at all. She was simply laying the groundwork for her reasons why she probably wouldn't renew his contract at the end of the fiscal year. He was tired, she would say, he seemed disengaged. Langley now knew this would be the argument.

When Maria and Orly left, Langley took his bottle of cabernet off the shelf and opened it. He put on a record by Dakota Stanton. In the dark of his living room, time seemed to float backward, he was drifting back in time, away from all this. He was in his Postwar Villa, protected by the *lares* and *penates,* deities of long-ago residents of the house. He was safe.

He stood in the dark, refilling his glass.

Church bells started to ring. The bells were from the Greek Orthodox Church. Langley had heard a rumor recently that it was going to shut down. Langley listened to the number of bells that rang. Suddenly, it was 11:00 o'clock.

In the morning, he put on his uniform and attended the press conference.

Only about half the media that had showed up on the first day were present. Most of them had moved on.

Ten

"Listen, my friend, this is a truly horrendous crime. It spans continents, governments, wildlife agencies, watchdog groups, conservationists, and we can't do much about that. You're talking about one animal," said Martin Poll, a biologist with the U.S. Fish & Wildlife Services when Langley asked him why he couldn't come to Fenton to speak to investigate the killing of the bird. Langley had him on the phone.

"But obviously, if it's here, it could mean ..."

"Let me give you a fact about animal trafficking," said Poll. "In Cyprus there is institutionalized killing of a songbird that makes for a kind of national delicacy. It's called ambelopoulia, and it's served in restaurants even though killing the bird is illegal in Cyprus."

Christ, Langley thought, he didn't want a lecture. He didn't want a history lesson.

"People give jars of the pickled bird as gifts. You see what I'm getting at?" Langley knew that Poll was trying to be helpful, but his curt manner and exasperated tone was frustrating. "Do you know where the most lucrative area for poaching these birds is on Cyprus? It's on a military base. So you see what we're up against."

"Yes," said Langley.

"We're talking about international efforts to oversee what are essentially localized problems, and the local people not only reject our oversight, they're disdainful of it, OK?"

"But this is happening here."

"In so many of these places the only way to make money is to poach a desired animal, you see? These are impoverished, desperate places. And there's a market."

"I get it," said Langley, quickly giving up trying to make his point.

"Governments look the other way, and the people who do this are regarded as patriotic because they're defying international authority, whether it's the E.U. or us," said Poll.

Langley sighed.

"We're talking millions and millions of animals. Not just birds but, well, you name it, and the money is staggering," he said. "And when we think we're just making some progress, along comes the Internet, and do you know that people are now buying and selling animals on the Internet? Ocelots. Tigers. Elephants. Do you know there are people buying and selling elephants on the Internet?"

"Christ," said Langley.

"I share your frustration, Chief Calhoun, I really do, but I don't have the resources to go after the big players. Imagine if I said I was going to Maine …"

"New Hampshire."

"… to investigate the death of a single bird. My funding would be shut off so fast I couldn't do anything," Poll said.

Eleven

A few days later Langley went to a pathology lab in Portsmouth to pick up the test results on the eagle, and everything was negative. He had taken the bird in a few days before. No toxins, no poison, no indication the bird had died of anything except violence. The report indicated the eagle was malnourished.

Langley read the report in the lobby of the lab. When he finished he asked the assistant behind the counter if the remains of the bird could be returned to him. She looked oddly at him and said quietly that she was certain the remains of the bird would have been destroyed.

This startled Langley for some reason. "Can you check with someone on that?"

"Well, sir, we sent the contents to a lab in Boston, and they did the tests there."

"Can you check for me, please?"

The woman eyed him once again, and she put a call through to the lab. "I have the Chief of Police from ...?" She looked at Langley for the answer.

"Fenton, New Hampshire."

"... New Hampshire. He was the one who brought the eagle in for testing, and he's asking for the remains." She listened. "That's what I told him." She sounded slightly annoyed. Langley's heart sank. She listened a little longer and then hung up. She turned to him. "I'm sorry, Sir, but the remains of the bird have been destroyed. That's simply according to the law."

It was something so obvious, and yet he had not expected it. He imagined the bird cut up, cut open, its blood smeared on a glass slide and placed under a microscope, and then simply tossed into a bin or a bag or a plastic container with a toxic symbol on the side.

But the bird wasn't toxic, it was perfectly harmless. It had been a living thing.

Langley thanked the woman and walked out of the lab. When he got to his car, the first person he thought of calling was Delia Reed, but he thought she was probably sick of hearing from him by now.

Maybe it was fitting. Maybe it was the perfect ending after all. No statement, no closure, no words, no thoughts, no sentiments, no resolution, no nothing.

The bird was just a little something that had caused a little trouble, and now it was over. Langley emailed the results to Martin Poll at Fish & Wildlife.

APRIL TURNED INTO MAY. No one was ever caught, and the incident faded. Other things were happening.

On Memorial Day, Langley's father picked up his son, and they drove into town.

Langley headed up the committee that was responsible for putting up the American flags and the bunting for the annual Memorial Day Parade. Every year he was reminded of just how many monuments, statues, granite memorials and plaques there were in Fenton for the young people who had died in wars. This did not include the number of veterans' graves in The Edge, the memorably creepy name that locals had given to the town cemetery more than a century ago.

There were also some new graves of the war dead from Fenton. These were bright, newly engraved stones, giving over to history the names of two young men who had been killed in action, one in Iraq and one in Afghanistan.

Langley thought that Main Street always looked stunning just before Memorial Day. Phone poles were decorated with new American flags. The porches on the older homes were decorated with red, white and blue bunting. There was a sign hanging on the bridge over Main Street that said Remember Staff Sgt. Bill Pierson, Nov. 18, 1989 - Jan. 3, 2010.

On the day they were putting up the flags, just a few days before the parade, Langley paired up with a pony-tailed former combat veteran from Vietnam named Herk Harvey who had the names of his fallen comrades sewn into the back of his jacket. Seven yellow triangles had the names of the dead and the dates they died. Herk Harvey didn't speak as they put up the flags, and Langley didn't try to engage him in conversation.

That guy has far more on his mind than I do, Langley said to himself. Timothy Calhoun had a similar jacket, which he also wore as he helped decorate the town.

There was one World War II vet, old Ira Stuertz, who still helped out. The remaining handful of soldiers and seamen and marines from that conflict showed up for the parade, either sitting in the back of a convertible in the parade, waving to a crowd newly appreciative of their sacrifice, or sitting on the sidelines. People applauded the soldiers as they walked by and shouted out, "Thank you for your service." Langley remembered a parade from fifteen years or so ago that had honored Gerry McLiesh, the last veteran from World War I. Gerry had just turned one hundred at the time, and he died the following fall.

Antonio Meli, a Korean War veteran, never wore his uniform and never had anything to do with the parade. He hated anything to do with war. Langley had heard Antonio tell a story once about how a young soldier from Maine had died in his arms. Antonio had been telling the story in a local restaurant, and Langley and his ex-wife Julia were sitting nearby and could hear the entire thing. Langley remembered the anguish in Antonio's voice, how quiet it became. He was talking to a young man in uniform.

Antonio was telling how he had pleaded with the young soldier not to die, to keep talking, and Langley and Julia stopped talking at their own table and listened. They couldn't help but listen. Antonio said he had kept asking the boy to say something, anything, to keep talking, but he had gone silent.

Antonio said the last words the kid said were, "Goddamn it." Langley wondered over the years, as he and Antonio became friends, if Antonio's frequent use of the phrase was meant to be some kind of tribute to that kid.

So Antonio always said he never had any reason to relive or celebrate the anniversary of his war.

Memorial Day came and went. The school year was coming to an end.

The reward check posted by Bill Plano went uncashed. The bird was forgotten by everyone, it seemed, until the residents of Fenton began thinking about their annual town meeting in late June, when they would vote on budget items and town warrants.

It was also the time, according to the town charter, when the chief of police would have his contract evaluated by the Board of Selectmen.

As the end of June approached, the postings on Fentonville.com started to speculate if Langley was the right man for the job. There was never any scandal, never any trouble, but he was being questioned.

"You have to stop reading that crap," his father said.

People were asking why he hadn't caught the people who killed the eagle. The unexplained fire and death of Carl Dieckmann from a few years before was resurrected.

Why didn't Chief Calhoun support the businesses in town that kept property taxes low?

One of the anonymous postings wondered if Langley was capable of keeping the town on an even keel. *Well, good for you, Brian,* Langley thought when he read that.

LANGLEY WENT INTO RUGGERIO'S MARKET on Summer Street to get the papers and a cup of coffee. He walked into the store and saw Ira Stuertz, who was pushing ninety. As usual, Ira was wearing his Marine Corps cap. It was worn and frayed, but once a jarhead, always a jarhead.

Langley watched Ira walk down the aisle. He saw the old man stop in front of a display of potted plants. Ira lived all by himself in a neat little house. His gardens out front were small and rectangular. Ira had a compact philosophy about life, which was this: Whenever you feel like dying, don't. So he didn't.

Ira was holding a small orange flower that was in a plastic green pot. It was the smallest, loneliest flower Langley had ever seen, and he wondered what Ira saw in it. He watched the old man put the pot in his carriage. Ira turned and started to resume his shopping when Langley walked up.

"Chief," Ira said exuberantly, and Langley was glad to hear his voice.

"Mr. Stuertz," said Langley. It was pronounced *stew-ertz.*

"Oh, they've got their blades out for you, boy," he said as they shook hands.

"So I understand."

"These old biddies," the old man said, looking around, seemingly implicating everyone in Ruggerio's Market. "Who the hell is going to keep us safe? Maria Tull? She can't see over the fucking dashboard." He whispered that last part for effect, and Langley laughed. "You won't be the first good chief they ran out of town on a rail."

"I'm not quite finished yet," said Langley.

"I used to work part-time at the town dump, did I ever tell you that?" Ira said suddenly.

"I don't think so."

"There was more shit happening there then you can imagine," he said, and Langley wondered what the point was. "You had all these guys there, and they're greeting everyone, saying hello, helping the old ladies with their bags of bottles, right? You can't imagine the sheer number of booze bottles we used to see on an hourly basis. This town is full of drunks. This was maybe 1975, '76. But the thing of it, all these guys, if someone came in and dropped off something they wanted, the place went nuts. A bed. A chest of drawers. An antique table, they'd kill themselves for it. They'd crack their heads open. Fist fights. At the town dump!"

"I'm not getting you, Ira."

He looked around conspiratorially. "The history of the town is written in that dump. All the stuff that people want kept hidden sees the light of day at a dump."

"And what does our dump say, Ira?"

"Everybody's crazy," he whispered, "so don't let it get you down."

"Thank you," said Langley. "I won't."

"I've been alive for ninety years," Ira said. But he didn't say anything else. Old Ira was on his way.

Langley shook his head and smiled. He bought the papers. He bought his coffee and his English muffin. He took a table and uncapped the coffee cup and looked at the front page of *The New York Times.* He was halfway through a story when he realized that no one had interrupted him.

He looked up, and there was no one around.

Twelve

Father's Day, Sunday, June 19. Langley went down to Hanscom's Bridge early in the morning with his spinner and a creel that Julia had given him years ago. He stopped by a small bait shack and bought some night crawlers. He was going to fish to just pass the time so he could get this miserable day over with.

Hanscom's Bridge was a covered span that had been given to the town about twenty years ago by the Chamber of Commerce. It crossed the Oquossoc and was meant to be a symbol of old New England. The walls of the bridge had large rectangular openings on each side allowing people to take a look out over the river and to fish.

Langley didn't really know how to fish. He could cast a mean line, but he had no idea what kind of bait to use or what kind of lure should be used for this or that kind of fish. His tackle box was filled with lures he had bought at yard sales over the years, and some of them were so old and unused the hooks were rusting and the plastic parts deteriorating. He had bought them to take his kids fishing, but now Langley never really went. On this Father's Day, on any Father's Day, he didn't really know what to do with himself.

He baited his hook with half a night crawler. He pushed the still squirming worm over the hook, reeled the line back in to the end of the rod, held the line down with his index finger, unlocked the spinner and gracefully cast out the line. The hook gently plopped into the flat water of the Oquossoc about a hundred feet out. The hook sank until the bobber stopped it from sinking farther, and Langley waited a few moments before he started to reel the line back in. The water was covered with pollen.

Langley pulled the hook out of the water and cast it out again. He put the rod down. He listened to the thwack and roll of the skateboarders that were riding in the skateboard park a few hundred yards down on the other side of the river.

The water seemed so quiet. Langley wondered if there were even any fish in it or if it was even the right time of day to fish. None of the other regulars were out. Maybe the old timers that really knew how to fish were driving by and looking at Langley and just shaking their heads.

His phone rang, and his niece Emily was on the other end of the line. "Happy Father's Day, Bigs," she said, and Langley could tell she was smiling.

"Emily Bean," he said, using his own nickname for her. "What's going on?"

"We're just getting ready to go to church."

"Well, I'm very happy you called. I'm just out trying to catch a fish."

"Have fun, Uncle Bigs."

"OK, Honey, thank you. Can I talk to Danny?"

"He's right here." The phone changed hands, and Danny said, "Happy Father's Day, Uncle Langley."

"Thank you, Danny. I'm just out here fishing right now, but maybe I'll stop by later on."

"I think I'm going to ride bikes with my friend Aaron."

"Have fun doing that, and I'll see you soon."

"OK, Uncle Langley, see you soon. Here's Dad."

"Happy Father's Day, old man," said Brian.

"Thank you, thank you. You, too. Any plans?"

"No, no. The kids are going off with their friends later, and I have to mow the lawn and do a few things. We're not doing anything special. What are you up to?"

"I'm just out fishing a little bit over here at Hanscom's."

"Trying to establish your bona fides with the locals?"

"No, I'm just ..."

"I'm just kidding. Listen, Eileen and I have to finish getting ready for church. Will we see you there?"

"I don't think so."

"Well, Happy Father's Day."

"You, too," said Langley, and he hung up his phone. He looked down into the Oquossoc.

Langley knew his own kids wouldn't call. The day before, he had received a card in the mail from the both of them. They had sent him a card that let them record their own voices, and they said simply, "Happy Father's Day." Nothing more than that. Not even, "Happy Father's Day, Dad." It was the most generic salutation possible.

Langley had half a mind to call Julia to ask why the kids even bothered anymore, but he realized that the reason for the call would not be to complain, but rather to have a chance to talk to the kids. Langley wanted to try to do something or say something that could repair the damage he had done.

But that was a tired scene, all this posturing. Besides, the father didn't do the calling on Father's Day. The father was the one who was supposed to get the call.

Thirteen

Langley was patrolling the town, as he did on occasion when the paperwork simply got to be too much or if he was too short-staffed to have anyone else go out. He was aimlessly driving through the town, half enjoying what he was seeing and half on the lookout for anything that might be wrong.

He was following a car that had a bumper sticker that read, If We Ignore the Environment, It Might Just Go Away."

Langley's phone buzzed, and when he picked it up he saw that it was Britney Sawuko calling from *The Fenton Herald.* Langley figured she was calling about the bird. There hadn't been anything about that for a while, and once in a while a reporter would call him just to check in to see if there was anything happening or if there were any updates on an old case.

He pulled over to pick up the call. He hated to drive when he spoke on the phone, because he was a regular speaker at the high school, telling teenagers the dangers of driving while distracted.

As Langley said hello, a slow-moving pickup truck drove by. Miller Lite cans were flying from its open bay. A clear plastic tarp looked like it was supposed to cover the back, but it flapped open in the wind. The cans were picked up in the draft and flung out onto the road.

"Chief Calhoun speaking."

"Chief, it's Britney from *The Herald*."

"Britney, I'm going to have to call you back." Langley pulled his vehicle out into the road and got behind the truck. A tin can popped out and went spinning underneath Langley's tires.

"Chief, I'm wondering if you know anything about Spiral Enterprises applying for a license to open up one of their stores in Fenton?"

Langley heard what she said, he knew what it meant, but then another Miller Lite can spun out from the back of the truck.

"Britney, I'm gonna have to call you back."

"Chief, I'm asking you if you know anything about Spiral Enterprises opening a new store in Fenton?"

"Britney, I'm about to pull someone over. I'm not ducking you. I'll call you back."

"If I don't hear from you …" But Langley had closed his phone and flipped on his siren and lights. The truck pulled over. In the driver's seat was a man named Art Hill. Langley nodded to Art and told him to get out his license and registration and then went to look in the back of the truck. Underneath the tarp were hundreds of Miller Lite cans.

"What's up, Chief?" Art said when Langley went back to the driver's side window. Art always squinted. He looked like he had the worst eyesight in the world, but he claimed it was merely a facial tic.

"Art, you're spewing beer cans all over the road."

Art twisted around to look at the back of his truck. "Sorry about that, Chief."

"The dump is open tomorrow morning. Why don't you go there and empty out the back of your truck."

"That's kind of embarrassing, Chief."

Langley looked at Art's documents and checked on his inspection sticker. "Well, embarrassing or not, I think you ought to get over there and empty your load, OK?"

"You got it, Chief."

Langley handed Art his license and registration. "Help me secure this tarp, will you?" Art hopped out of the cab, and the two of them tightened up the cover. He let Art go on his way, saying that if he hadn't emptied his truck the next time he saw him, he'd cite Art, and he'd have to a pay a fine.

"I'll do it in the morning, Chief."

"Thank you," Langley said and got back in his car. He drove up the road and pulled off onto a shoulder that gave enough room for other cars to get by.

He looked at his phone and didn't know whether to call Britney back or call his brother. Brian was the attorney for Spiral Enterprises, which owned a chain of adult entertainment stores. There were always rumors about those places. The name of the chain was simply Dirty Books, and there were maybe two dozen of them up and down the East Coast.

Brian had been a member of its legal team for the past five or six years, and Langley thought—he assumed—that Brian, out of some sort of familial loyalty or respect for the town, wouldn't bring that kind of business into Fenton. He was wrong, apparently.

Langley knew he couldn't call Brian. If he did and Brian confirmed it, he couldn't tell Britney he didn't know anything about it. Not knowing about it also meant that Brian hadn't even had the courtesy to call him, to inform the Chief of Police of this move, and that would make

Langley look like he was out of touch with his family and the town. He also did not want to have Britney write that he did not return her calls. He dialed her number.

"Hi, this is Britney."

"Britney, Chief Calhoun."

"Thank you for calling me back."

"I know this won't be satisfactory, but I can't have any comment on that now. I just can't comment."

"Oh, Chief, come on. This is right in your backyard in every sense of the word."

"But it's a—off the record—it's a ... did you hear what I said?"

"This is off the record."

"Are we clear on that?"

"You only have to say it once, Chief."

"It's a legal business. It's perfectly within their rights."

"But Chief, I know that you've gone before the Zoning Board how many times in the past five years or so to ask them to amend the current zoning regulations so that this kind of business wouldn't be allowed." She was right about that. "They didn't listen, and now ..."

For four of those years Brian Calhoun had served on the Zoning Board, all perfectly legal, all perfectly above board.

"Britney, I can't say anything."

"How do you think the town is going to react when your brother helps bring a franchise into town that nobody is going to want?"

"I doubt that nobody is going to want it," Langley said. He shook his head and smiled. People may publicly say they don't want that kind business, but once it opened it would do all right. Then, as though he was afraid Britney had just read his thoughts, "This entire conversation is off the record."

"Do you want this type of business in Fenton? Personally? Do you want it?"

She was really riding him. "No comment," was all he said before he disconnected. He didn't like doing that, but he had to.

He was sitting in his vehicle on the side of the road near one of the old working farms in Fenton. When Langley looked out across the fields, still covered with brown stubble from last year's corn harvest and with no cars or machinery in sight, just two tall silos built maybe sixty or seventy years ago at the far end of the field and a nice tight red barn filled with hay, Langley realized that he could have been looking at a scene from 1940 or 1950 or 1960. He doubted that this view had changed much at all in all that time.

"Goddamn it," Langley said out loud. "*Goddamn*."

Fourteen

Salmon Falls, New Hampshire, was about twenty minutes from Fenton. There was a Dirty Books store in that town, and Langley was going to take a look at it. He drove into the parking lot knowing full well there was a security camera somewhere catching him on tape.

The store looked like the one they were going to build in Fenton, a square box, one story tall, no windows, a backlit sign out front on a steel pole.

There was a sign out front advertising smoke accessories. Langley wondered how the porno business was actually doing, given how much free stuff there was online. It suddenly struck him as a funny business to be getting into. No one bought DVDs or CDs any more. People just downloaded everything.

The name of the store, Dirty Books, seemed absurd, silly really. There were little gold stars bursting around the name on the sign, and there was a tagline, The Time of Your Life. The name of the porn store in Portsmouth when Langley was growing up was the Blue Moon Reader. At least there had been some attempt at giving the name some romanticism. Now it was simply the Dirty Books store.

It was a sunny day. Langley drove around the back of the store to where the dumpster was and looked inside, but it had been recently emptied. The parking lot looked clean, pretty well swept up—recently swept up. He got back into his car and went out to the main drag and took a left down a side street that went right behind the store. He was looking for someone to talk to when he saw a woman out in her garden, raking up the remnants of her mums.

"Excuse me," Langley said, getting out of his car. Over time he had learned how to walk up to someone so they wouldn't be alarmed and put up their guard just at the moment he was going to ask them some questions. He smiled and waved. "Hi," he said. 'I'm just curious. Can I ask you a quick question?"

By this time he was on her lawn. "I'm Langley Calhoun, I'm Chief of Police in Fenton, and we just learned they're going to put one of these stores in our town. I wanted to find out about it."

"Oh, that," said the woman.

"We just found out they're putting one on Route 136, and we had a town meeting about it, and people aren't too happy," he said.

"Can you imagine trying to sell your house with that thing right next door?" she said, looking over at the building. "I don't care what they do inside there, but we're stuck. I'll be lucky if my kids want my house, even if I tell them I'm going to give it to them."

"Does the business cause any trouble?"

"Not really," she said. "I mean, it's quiet for the most part. Sometimes the parking lot overflows, and people park out here on the street."

"Seems like such a small building to have overflow parking."

"Like I said," she said, "I don't care what goes on inside there. I just want my neighborhood quiet."

Langley looked around. "What does go on in there?"

"A bunch of us went to the police a long time ago. You can read about this place on the Internet. People actually rate these kinds of places. Four stars. Two thumbs up, you know."

"Rate it for sexual activity?"

"What do you think?"

Langley just shook his head.

"Men go in there," she said. "It's like a rest stop. They pull in, go inside, do their business, leave."

"Christ," said Langley.

"Christ is right."

"Have you ever met the owner?" he asked.

"I don't want to meet the owner. You always hear all kinds of things. Mafia, you know. You hear enough rumors that make you scared, so you don't want to do anything. It makes you afraid," she said. "Are you going to do anything about it?"

"I don't know if we can."

"Of course not," said the woman, disgusted. "Why should there be laws that actually help anybody."

Langley just shook his head. "Thank you," he said.

"Good luck," she said.

"BRIAN?"

"Hey, Langley."

"I got a call from a reporter over at *The Fenton Herald* a little while ago."

"How nice for you. Are they still on this bird thing?" Brian was on speaker phone, and he seemed out of breath.

"Oh, no, they've moved on from that. They're now interested in Dirty Books."

"Really?"

"Yes, really."

"What did you say?"

"What could I say? I said no comment."

"Good."

Langley was distracted by his brother's heavy breathing. "What's the matter?"

"I'm on the treadmill."

"When did you start working out on a treadmill?"

"Ever since Dad had his heart attack. I figured it was a wake-up call."

"For Dad. You seem like you're in pretty good shape."

"Not according to federal guidelines. I'm obese."

"Do you want me to call you back?"

"No, no. Listen, I don't have much to say. We're going to file the paperwork, go through the process. There's a site in the business district on 136 that's good."

"You're just determined to turn Route 136 into some kind of paradise, aren't you?"

"Listen, Langley, it's the town's business district. I know you'd rather turn it into a Victory Garden or something."

"But a pornographic video store?"

"It's adult entertainment."

"Oh, please. Come on."

"We're not putting it in a neighborhood. It's not near a school, any of that."

"But you could have, I mean ..."

"What?"

"... told me about it."

"And then I would tell my clients what, exactly, Langley?"

"I wouldn't have done anything about it."

"I don't know what you're squawking about. I did you a favor. Plausible deniability never hurt any law enforcement officer."

"Nice."

"Is that it? I can't do this and talk at the same time."

"Just keep me updated."

"You'll read about it in the paper like everybody else. See ya."

Brian hung up.

Fifteen

Langley was furious.

He had seen this time and time again. It's a fact of life that small towns in New England have been constantly caught off guard by the modern world.

When Langley used to speak before the zoning board and ask them to tighten up the town's zoning ordinances, he said that Fenton's laws were so vague that anyone could put almost any kind of business anywhere they wanted.

"You need to clarify the laws concerning what you can put near schools, around parks, around churches, or we're going to find ourselves in trouble," Langley said, but no one listened, least of all his brother Brian, who was sitting twenty feet in front of Langley as a member of the Zoning Board.

Langley knew he had overstepped his bounds with these boards because he had become too preachy. He was correct, but he had become too preachy and self-righteous.

"Just keeping the main intersection in town free of a traffic light doesn't automatically mean that the town hasn't changed or that the people moving in will still be courteous or polite or even respect these old traditions," he told the Zoning Board. "People will inevitably come in and change it."

Langley remembered the smile on Brian's face and how he had wondered at the time what it meant. When Bill

Plano and his business partners came to town not very long after, Langley knew exactly what Brian's enigmatic smile meant.

Plano's company bought the land and filed papers. They appeared before the necessary boards. They promised the landfill operation would be quiet. "You would hardly even know it's there," Bill Plano told the paper.

Ah, thought Langley, *if you don't see it, then the town doesn't really change.*

When Langley saw Brian out one night at the local tavern, he told him there were half a dozen reasons why the Zoning Board could turn away the business.

"It's out of my hands," Brian said. Langley asked what that meant. "What it means is that I've resigned from the Planning Board because Bill Plano is now a client."

Langley knew that Brian was able to exploit every loophole, every outdated ordinance that was on Fenton's books. Langley knew that his brother looked at Fenton not as a town but as a client, a business location, a place to make some good money.

It was this way in town after New England town, year after year, when people were suddenly faced with having to approve the application for pornographic bookstores or strip joints or widened roads or any of the other so-called developments they didn't really want.

Langley remembered when Benham Road needed to be widened. Benham Road used to be wide enough for Ira Stuertz's father's wagon to drive in one direction and for a car or buggy to pass going the other way. If they slowed down, they could squeeze by each other just fine.

But Benham Road was no longer wide enough for the SUVs driving in both directions. It was no longer wide enough for SUVs and for the joggers running along the side of the road with baby carriages. Residents would call the police department and say, "Somebody's going to get killed out there."

Then one day a baby carriage being pushed by its jogging mother was almost sideswiped. The outraged parent called Langley and said the baby was almost hit and the road wasn't wide enough, and what was he going to do about it?

Langley told the jogger to go before the Board of Selectmen, which she did by hiring an attorney to do their talking for them. They made an appeal to widen the road. Their neighbors agreed. Then there was a new bond issue question put on the warrant at the next year's town meeting asking to borrow funds to widen Benham Road.

The bond was approved, and the road was widened. Property taxes went up, but the farmers who hadn't had a raise in pay in decades could no longer pay the tax, so their farms were sold. New houses were built on that land, and more taxes were needed for town services for those new families. There was now even more traffic on Benham Road, and people began to wonder if they had actually widened it enough.

Enter A & J Landfill—and now Dirty Books—to solve all your tax needs.

When Langley called Maria Tull to ask if she knew about the application for the Dirty Books franchise, she told him to mind his own business.

"I'm here to follow the law, and you're here to enforce it," she said. "You're not here to make the laws, Chief, but maybe you've forgotten that."

She, too, hung up on him.

Maybe if you ignore Fenton, it will just go away, Langley thought to himself.

Sixteen

Non-Public Board of Selectmen Session, Wednesday, June 22 , 7:00 p.m. Langley knew Brian was actively, if covertly, seeking his ouster as Chief, something Brian denied when he was asked by both Langley and their father. But Langley knew he was out anyway, and he didn't feel like fighting any more.

Langley wondered briefly about the mental state of his brother. He could understand having their differences. He could tolerate their long periods of estrangement. But he could not fathom why his brother was truly trying to upset his life and his livelihood.

People told Langley they supported him when they saw him. "We're with you, Chief," they all said cheerfully, but Langley knew.

The local paper ran an editorial in support of continuing the contract, but in the following Sunday paper Bill Plano had an op-ed stating his reasons why the chief should go. Langley submitted his budget. At $3.55 million it was a modest increase over the current year's allocation, but it would be shot down by the Selectmen, he was sure of that.

Langley usually wore his uniform to contract negotiations, but tonight he wore a jacket with an open collar shirt. He was relaxed. He called his attorney, Chleo Brooke, and asked her to meet him at the municipal building just before 7:00. There was no need to go through anything beforehand.

"You're sure?" she asked.

"We're good," said Langley.

She asked Langley what it was he intended to do, and he simply said, "Get in and out as fast as I can." When he arrived at the municipal offices just before 7:00, the breeze was balmy and the stars were out.

Maria Tull gaveled the meeting into session right on time. She had such a stern look on her face that Langley leaned over to Chleo and said, "I'm gonna have to get a new dentist."

The meeting was not open to the public because it was a personnel matter. Those deliberations are always private. All five members of the Board were present, plus the Town Clerk, Pat Dilley, who was there to record the minutes, as well as the town's legal counsel, Eb Webb. Eb had on a sporty bow tie. Even Maria looked unusually officious.

"How are you, Chief?" she asked as he sat at the table that had been positioned to face the board. Langley wanted to say simply, "Oh, let's cut out the bullshit," but he said that he was fine and asked how the Chairman was. Maria said she was fine.

"Thank you for taking the time to meet with us tonight, Chief. As you know, as mandated by the Fenton town charter, we're required to give you a fair review of your job performance at the end of each three-year contract and to submit to you what we feel is a fair offer for your continued services. We are also not in any way obligated to continue your employment as Chief of Police in Fenton, located in Rockingham County, New Hampshire."

They sure are enjoying this, Langley thought. This private little party was one of the few times these people could exercise any of the so-called power they felt should come with being an elected official, and by God they were going to exercise it.

Day after day, in meeting after meeting, Langley knew that these poor elected folks have to sit there and take it from the few crackpots that actually show up at their meetings. They have to endure being called too liberal or too conservative or too ineffectual. They spend their time approving victual licenses, summarizing expenditures, debating whether a stop sign should be put at the intersection of Penhallow and Brixham Roads. They debate whether the town dump hours should be extended and whether the library ought to cut back on its days of operation. They agonize over whether they can afford a new patrol car.

That the Board of Selectmen, for the most part, did a pretty good job of spending the taxpayers' money prudently seemed to be the least satisfying thing they did, even though it was the most important.

Langley could see their frustration oozing out of them. Since they were elected by the people, that elected office ought to come with some power. It ought to feel like they are in power, and too often they felt like clerks. Langley knew they weren't going to feel like clerks on this night. This was the one institutionalized moment when they could exercise the power they felt they were owed, and they were going to enjoy it. Isn't that what running for public office was about?

"Chief Calhoun, before we begin, do you have anything to say?"

"No, Chairman, not at this time."

Langley could feel a little of their hot air escape. When he was first appointed chief, he was stepping in for the previous chief, who had taken a job with the newly elected governor. That was a little more than eight years ago. In the two subsequent hearings on his contract renewals, Langley had made heartfelt statements about how he loved the job, loved working for the people of Fenton, and how he was proud to serve the town.

He knew if he made such a statement this year, any innocent remark, anything along the lines of how he had tried his utmost to uphold the decency and the standards of Fenton, some member of the Board would end up saying that it was "all good and well to try, Chief, but sometimes trying isn't enough."

He wasn't going to give them any rope to hang him with. So when he declined to speak, the smirks and the self-satisfied postures drooped a little.

"I'm sure the Chief has his reasons for being silent," said Red Richardson. Langley had to give it to him. Old Red found a way to zing him nonetheless. Langley almost leaned over to Chloe to tell her that he was leaving, but something somewhere inside of him switched on and suggested that he just sit back and enjoy the show.

Chairman Tull had two stacks of letters in front of her. "As you know, Chief, we allow the public to weigh in on your performance, and as you know we are obligated under our charter to factor in public good will to the current office holder in our deliberations. How we do so is solely up to our discretion."

She picked up a stack, and Langley saw that her hands were shaking. Officially, all Maria Tull had to do was ask that each and every letter be entered into the public record and then move on. But what she decided to do was to read the names of each letter writer out loud. She was really going to drag this out. After she read a few names in support of the chief, Chloe Brooke stood and said, "The Chief fully appreciates any citizen who took the time to write in, regardless of their views, and we fully accept that the Town will faithfully enter each letter that has been submitted into the public record and to consider it appropriately."

Maria Tull, in full opera mode, thanked Chloe and then continued to read the names of the people who felt Langley should keep his job. Antonio Meli was among those who supported the Chief. Brian Calhoun was not among those represented.

When Maria read the names of the people critical of the chief's performance, she read out Bill Plano's name. When Langley read Plano's letter much later, he knew it might as well have been signed by Brian Calhoun. Almost thirty minutes later, she had read all the names, for and against.

Maria then segued into the part on the agenda when the other four members of the Board could comment and ask the Chief questions. This was ostensibly the time when the Chief would take the opportunity to parry with the Selectmen to defend his performance.

Orly Bigelow had just opened his mouth when Chloe stood and asked for a vote on the status of the Chief's contract without any further deliberation.

"Chief Calhoun feels that the members of the Board have already formed an opinion as to whether Chief Calhoun should continue in his current position. Chief Calhoun believes fully that his performance speaks for itself. You know the statistics of crime in this town, you know the rate of convictions, and you know his status among the townspeople—outside of the bundled letters with negative opinions from employees of A & J Fill & Gravel."

Everybody on the Board got their backs up a little when she said that, but Chloe had done her homework. "And you know Chief Calhoun's personal commitment. If you feel, and this is certainly within your rights, that it is time for new blood, for another point of view, then the Chief is fully prepared to accept the opinion put forth by the board. Thank you." Chloe started to sit down, then stood up again. "If the Board insists on continuing the discussion about the performance of the Chief, I will ask him to leave the proceedings and I, as his counsel, will witness the expressions from the Board and accept them all as they stand. Thank you again." That really did it.

When Orly Bigelow said he was really sorry to hear that, Langley knew that Orly didn't mean that he was sorry he wasn't able to castigate the Chief. He was sorry that small town politics had gotten in the way of a good man continuing his job. At any rate, that was the way Langley figured it, because Orly was the only one to vote in favor of continuing his contract.

With a vote of four to one, which seemed to Langley such an insignificant number no matter how you cut it, he would be out of a job on June thirtieth.

WHEN EVERYONE MET LATER at the Foreside Bar & Grill—and everyone was there including the Selectmen, the lawyers, the Town Clerk—Langley accepted the well-wishes of the people who had just ousted him. He looked around the pub and saw Chloe in deep conversation with Eb Webb.

Red Richardson was sitting next to Langley blabbing about something. Langley wasn't listening. He looked around and saw Fred Amsell and a few other people in town that he knew, and suddenly he realized he was going to miss his job. He would miss it, but he wouldn't agonize over its loss.

He had applied for his private investigator's license, just in case, and that was expected to come through any day. He had also lined up some freelance work from some attorneys he knew. With his pension, with some new work and less responsibility, he thought there was a chance he could get by all right.

Langley felt as though he ought to call his ex-wife and let her know what was happening, but he couldn't open his phone to call.

He felt slightly better when his father showed up. The old man was clearly already blitzed. His unsure gait was being steadied by a beautiful black woman who Langley assumed was the object of his father's affections.

Seventeen

Friday, July 3. "But I'm not a cop anymore," Langley said into the phone.

"I know, I know, but you boys in blue, you always stick together, right?"

"I don't know, Freddie, maybe we'd better not this year."

"Oh, my God, and lose by default? I don't think so. Come on, I'll pick you up at four, OK?"

Four meant 4:00 a.m. Langley hesitated.

"You've got to do it for our side," said Freddie Ouillette.

"All right, pick me up."

"That's my man."

At 4:00 a.m., Langley and Freddie were on I-95 in Freddie's pickup, heading south to Pennsylvania to buy fireworks. It was pitch black. Freddie wanted some impressive explosions this year because, even though last year was generally believed to be a tie, he felt that he had lost the fireworks contest held in town every year.

Freddie Ouillette had inadvertently started one of Fenton's most popular annual events. Twelve or thirteen years ago he had gone down to the banks of the Oquossoc, just across from Sam Sifton's house, and set off some fireworks on the night before July 4th. Freddie had been drunk at the time, and he lit off a dozen bottle rockets and a few packs of salutes.

"Take that, Sifton!" he yelled to the house across the river, and that was how it started.

Sam Sifton and Freddie Oiullette were friends, even though they owned rival bars up in York Beach. Sam had a big house on the other side of the Oquossoc, and he had his own tradition. On the night of July 3rd Sam always had a big bonfire. Freddie wanted to compete a little bit, so he lit off the bottle rockets. There was no one else on the river bank that first night except Freddie and his girlfriend at the time.

"You're a crazy bastard!" Sam Sifton yelled back that first year.

So the next year Freddie and Sam both brought fireworks and exchanged blasts on their sides of the river. It started modestly but had grown in size and danger each successive year. Crowds started to show up and vote on who they thought had the best display.

When the whole town got involved, Langley always asked a couple of his officers to go down to the river to keep an eye on things. There was always a lot of drinking. Langley couldn't work the detail because he had been unofficially named Freddie's pyrotechnics assistant early on and was never on duty that night. That's what Freddie called him. "You're my pyrotechnics assistant."

Freddie started to buy his fireworks in Pennsylvania. A few years ago, he called up Langley and asked him to drive down to Philadelphia with him. "That's where the industrial stuff is," Freddie said. He said he needed police protection when he brought the explosives across state lines. Langley had been going with Freddie now for years.

This year, Freddie said he was planning on buying something like a thousand dollars worth of fireworks.

Freddie and Langley made it down and back from Pennsylvania without incident. Freddie's open can of Bud Light in the car on the way home made Langley more nervous, in fact, than the boxes of fireworks in the back.

When they got back to Fenton, Freddie took Langley into his garage. "I want to show you something. This is what Bob Francis made for me."

Freddie picked up a heavy piece of metal that had four short, open-ended steel pipes sticking up from a thick square base. "This is the platform," said Freddie solemnly. "I can light four bombs at once. Sifton won't know what hit him."

LATER THAT NIGHT, everyone in Fenton drifted down to the town's boat launch, which was at the narrowest section of the Oquossoc. Sam Sifton already had his bonfire going, and he was playing the Rolling Stone's "Tattoo You" loudly on his sound system. The music echoed across the river.

It was about nine o'clock. It was getting dark, and the adults were carrying their favorite drinks, and the kids were running around with sparklers.

People were greeting Langley warmly. Langley saw Brian and his family, but he didn't go over to speak to them. Delia, who was with a friend, some guy that Langley did not know, came over to him.

"Hey," she said.

"Hi," Langley said.

"I was sorry to hear about how the Selectmen handled your situation," she said.

"I expected it," said Langley, placing the box of explosives on top of a cinder block to keep them dry. He suddenly realized that she was not simply making an observation. She was saying she felt as though he had been hurt. "Thank you," he said.

After a pause, she said, "Are you going to stay in town?"

"Oh, God, yes," said Langley. "Did someone tell you that I wasn't?"

"No, no, I just figured after what happened, you know, that ..."

"No, no. I'm staying put."

She looked at Langley. She was holding her hands behind her back, sort of stretching her arms out, and she looked tense and awkward. It was at this event about four or five years ago that Langley first met Delia.

"I guess the whole bird thing has faded away," she said.

Langley smiled. He knew that the very people who wanted the incident of the bird to go away without resolution were the very people who had written to the town and cited his lack of progress on it as one of the reasons why his contract shouldn't have been renewed.

He was fiddling stupidly with the fireworks. She stood there while Langley was bent over the box, looking for whatever they were going to light first.

"Langley," Delia said, and she said it so sharply that he looked up. "Call me," she said.

He only nodded as she drifted back into the crowd.

Langley held the flashlight as Freddie lit four fuses with a lighter. The Roman candles burst apart in the sky above the river. Their reflections in the smooth water made the explosions seem double in size. Sparks floated down from the sky and sizzled out in the water.

"Whaddya think of that, Sifton?" Freddie yelled, his voice echoing off the surface of the water. He was certainly drunker than he ought to have been.

"You're a pussy," came the reply from behind the bonfire on the other side.

They exchanged volleys. Every time a new set of fireworks went off, spectators on both sides of the river clapped, and everyone laughed. The back-and-forth lasted about an hour. The applause for each side seemed equitable.

"Now, for the *pièce de résistance,*" said Freddie to Langley. He had bought two squat canisters that looked like the barrels of a Gatling gun. Each canister had fifty tubes housing an individual rocket. The woman in Pennsylvania who sold it to him said it was one of their most popular brands. It was called the New York Harbor Celebration. Each one cost fifty dollars.

Langley set each one near the water and told everyone to get back. He and Freddie expected a monumental display. Freddie lit the fuses. For the next five minutes the Sifton side of the river watched with the delighted realization that these particular fireworks were a monumental failure. They laughed and applauded as tiny sparkles fizzled and hissed out of the canisters, none of which leapt higher than three feet.

Freddie kept throwing his arms up and shouting, "Is that all it does? Is that all there is?" He hated to lose, but he was going to lose this year. He was mortified. As the sparkles sputtered out, the applause from the Sifton camp got louder and louder. The folks on the Fenton side of the river even had to applaud. It was the loudest applause of the night, but everyone knew on Freddie's side that they were beat.

"You're making this too easy, Freddie!" yelled Sam.

Then everyone in Fenton saw four or five people scramble down to a small dock on the other side of the river. They watched as five lighters flared up, and a true, blazing fireworks display ended the evening. Everyone clapped and laughed. The last few sparkles drifted silently down from the sky, and all seemed suddenly empty and quiet. There was the smell of sulfur in the air.

"Goodnight, Freddie," Sam yelled. "Happy Independence Day."

"Happy Fourth, Sammy," Freddie shouted back.

Then everyone turned away from the water. A hush had fallen over the crowd. There was a lovely, contented feeling in the air as they walked back up the streets to their cars. They held hands and held their children. Someone was playing "America the Beautiful" on a trumpet off in the distance. It could have come from either side of the river. It didn't matter.

A feeling of community and relaxation hung in the Fenton air. As the crowd began to spread out to their separate homes, neighbors smiled and nodded to each other as a way to say goodbye. It was as though they had left their voices down at the river, and speaking would break the spell. The night was hot and liquid.

Langley looked across the crowd and saw Brian carrying little Emily, who was fast asleep in his arms. He saw Delia and her friend walking up the hill. He craned his neck to see if they were holding hands or walking arm in arm, but it was too dark to see.

He didn't turn on the lights when he entered The Postwar Villa. He slipped off his shoes and instinctively went to his belt to remove his gun, which of course was not there, and he went into his bedroom and stretched out on top of the blankets.

His little town was falling asleep all around him, and he fell asleep to the sounds of that.

Eighteen

On July 7, one week after his contract ended, Langley's private detective's license arrived in the mail, and two days later he was sitting in the office of Ed Lustig, a Manchester attorney who handled divorce cases. Langley had needed to get out of Fenton, to do something else, to spend time with people he didn't already know. So he found himself facing Ed Lustig across his desk.

Everything about Lustig was gray. His hair was gray, his skin was gray, his eyes were gray, his office was gray. He was obscured by a cloud of gray cigarette smoke.

"I love tobacco," he said without being prompted, "Any kind of tobacco."

Langley was waiting for Lustig to tell him what to do.

"I have a guy who is claiming his ex-wife is abusing their special needs child," said Lustig, throwing a manila folder across the desk to Langley. "His name is Alfred Ramos. The wife's name is Virginia Ramos, and they have one child, Ramon, who is autistic. You ever hear of Munchausen Syndrome by proxy?"

"It's where a parent or guardian deliberately makes someone sick so they can make a hero of themselves by taking care of them."

"Alfred Ramos is convinced that his wife is hurting their autistic child deliberately. The kid has bruises, that kind of thing. But since the kid doesn't speak and never indicates any kind of fear or hostility to the mother, or any kind of emotion, we have to find some direct evidence."

"Is Ramos really convinced it's his wife, or is he simply trying to pin something on her to make her life miserable?" asked Langley as he looked at photos of the injured child, a boy of about seven with dark hair. The bruises on the child repulsed him.

"Someone is hurting the child. The cops have been involved, social services. The mother denies everything."

"Has she accused the husband of doing this instead?"

"Not even a hint. She doesn't say too much." Lustig was turning his cigarette in his big round ashtray. He was molding the red hot ash at the end of the cigarette into a long cone. "I want you to follow her and the kid around, see what you can see."

"The couple is divorced?"

"Couple years now."

"How long do we keep up the surveillance?"

"I mean, if we follow them around for a few weeks and something happens, great. Not great, but you know what I mean. If nothing happens we tell the father that he can keep paying us, but why?" Lustig was stubbing out his cigarette. "Three weeks. Thousand a week for three weeks."

"Good," said Langley.

"She has the kid during the week, and the father takes him on Wednesdays and every Saturday and Sunday," said Lustig lighting up another smoke. Langley had quit smoking a year before, but he reflexively took the cigarette that was offered him and lit up.

Nineteen

Langley hadn't spent much time in Manchester, New Hampshire. It struck him like any other small American city. It was schizophrenic. Some parts of it were beautiful, gorgeous. Some of it was less beautiful. There were museums and there were dive bars. There were elegant old homes and flophouses. There were new buildings made entirely of steel and glass. There were buildings of crumbling brick. It had a great little ballpark where the Fisher Cats played. There were first class restaurants, as well as convenience stores that made their money selling nothing but booze and cigarettes and lottery tickets to the indigent. There were civic organizations and gangs.

The downtown had definitely been hit by the Great Recession. People loitered about, waiting for something to happen. There was trash gently being blown down Elm Street. The cops looked serious, thought Langley. They were on their toes. That was always a sign the economy was in the dumps. People are volatile when they have no money.

Langley had introduced himself to the Chief of Police and to some of the police detectives. A few of them casually knew Langley. He had met some of them at conventions and seminars over the years. When he was out on the street following Virginia Ramos, he would tell a beat cop who he was, just so they would know why he was hanging around. He'd be carrying a camera and taking some pictures, but he was obviously no tourist.

On his fourth day on the job, Langley was leaning against a lamppost and smoking. That he was smoking at all amazed and disappointed him, but it was a useful diversion when all he had to do most of the time was wait around.

He was watching Virginia Ramos, who was a lovely young woman, as she carefully walked down the street with her seven-year-old boy. The kid hadn't fallen down. He wasn't clumsy in a way that could account for the bruises, and she hadn't been negligent with Ramon in any way. Not even in a sly, cunning way.

But Ramon was also clearly a lost child. Langley thought of his own children, about whom he seemed to think constantly now. Spending so much time watching someone else's child, even though it was for a job, made him feel guilty. He hadn't spent a total of two days with his own children in the past several years. It was a miserable record.

Langley's children were resentful, and he was wondering how much he had hurt them. He wondered how much this hurt was being repaired by Julia's new husband. The conversations with his children were getting shorter and shorter. He hoped that their feelings of resentment hadn't yet metastasized into hatred. Maybe they had. Maybe he didn't know the depths of their feelings.

He had to stop daydreaming. Virginia and Ramon had drifted farther down the street, and he was losing them. He quickly followed. Something had happened that he had missed. Virginia was leaning over, trying to explain something to the child, but it wasn't clear if the boy understood. He had a blank expression on his face. Langley took out his camera and took a few photos. It looked as though Virginia Ramos was getting agitated. If she was going to do something to hurt Ramon, it would be in a situation like this.

She leaned in close. She lifted her hand but put it gently on the boy's shoulder. Her mouth was contorted, and she was straining to explain something. Ramon stood there, a statue. She dropped her hand and took his little hand in hers, and they started down the street again. Nothing happened, and Langley suddenly felt relieved that she had not done anything violent.

He had begun to think that Virginia Ramos was attractive. He hadn't thought so at first, but as he looked at her he began to see the beauty in her face, the shape of her body, and the way she dressed. His first impression was that she was one of those people who didn't care how she looked, but a couple of times she had come out of the house and gone right back in to change a blouse or a pair of jeans. She was slender and elegant. Her looks were probably the one thing she had control over, Langley thought.

He took more photos and smiled silently to himself. As he scrolled through the photos he had already taken, he knew he was a sad romantic. He was also lonely. He sighed. Forget about it. What was he going to do anyway? This was going to be just a job, and he had to prove himself because he wanted to work more with Ed Lustig.

Langley followed Virginia and her child in their car, and he sat outside their small, nondescript home. He watched through the windows with binoculars as the boy sat and watched television and Virginia sat on the couch next to him, talking on the phone.

She was having an animated conversation, one that quickly turned so heated she left the room. Ramon sat there with a faraway look in his eyes as though he didn't hear anything at all.

LANGLEY WAS UPLOADING HIS PHOTOS into a file when Lustig came in and asked how it was going.

"Slow," said Langley. "I haven't seen anything. Well, let me say that there were a couple of times when I saw the woman frustrated and agitated, and she didn't make a move. I don't think that child is in any danger."

"It's only been a week," said Lustig.

"It's just that I haven't seen anything."

"No chance you've been noticed?"

"I don't think so. She acts completely natural."

"Good, good," said Lustig, rolling an unlighted cigarette between his fingers.

"I see her talking on the phone every night. Pretty angry. Is that with the husband?"

"They hate each other, so he tells me. I don't talk to her."

"I see no boyfriend or friends, no one else who could be hurting the child. She seems alone."

Lustig only shrugged his shoulders. He was sitting on a couch reading Maxim.

"Where does Ramos live?"

Lustig rattled off the address. "The guy's my client. What do you need to know for?"

"I just want to get a look at the guy, that's all," said Langley.

Twenty

Langley usually drove home about 2:00 a.m. At the end of every day he and Lustig would go out for a cocktail and talk. They were two people with nowhere to go, so they talked about the law and law enforcement, and Lustig asked Langley if private investigator work was really what he wanted to do.

"I like it, so far," said Langley.

"You ought to be in the Peace Corps or something," said Lustig.

Langley snorted. "Why do you say that?"

"I don't know, but you should be in the Peace Corps," he said.

There was nobody on I-95 at this hour except long-haul tractor trailers and logging trucks. Langley drove with the window down and leisurely puffed on a cigarette. "Goddamn Lustig," he said out loud. He had never wanted another cigarette in his life.

He turned on the radio and listened to a BBC report about the theft of honey bees in Japan, and he was wide awake when he turned into his driveway.

He turned on the light in his small living room, the first room in the house that you walked into. There was a couch, a few simple tables, a standing lamp with colorful plastic covers over the bulbs. There was a picture of his family—his wife and kids and himself—on the wall, the four of them standing in front of a Christmas tree. Langley couldn't remember what year it had been taken.

He walked straight through to the kitchen and reached for his wine and poured some into a jam jar and added the ice cube and seltzer. The wine burned his throat. It was cheap wine. He put another cube in the glass. He didn't like to drink anything warm unless it was coffee or tea.

Langley pulled a chair out from the kitchen table and sat. It was dark, and the streets outside were quiet. It was the time of the morning when almost no one was awake. There wasn't a light on in a house for miles. People were either sleeping soundly or lying awake in a fit of insomnia, worrying about whatever it was they had done. Langley didn't feel like sleeping at all.

He thought about the Christmas when that picture had been taken. His daughter Patty looked about three, and Annie was about five. When was that, five, six years ago? Just before Christmas. They were twice that old now. Langley had missed almost half their lives.

He had always tried to make Christmas a memorable time for his kids. He remembered the Christmases with his mother and father, how the house always had the aroma of cinnamon or pine needles. He remembered how the spirit of Christmas seemed a very real, palpable thing. His parents always tried to make Christmas the best time of year for Brian and Langley. Sometimes they tried too hard.

Langley and the girls used to hang decorations inside the house and out in the yard. The children really loved the lighted Christmas tree in the middle of the back yard. The images Langley had in his head of looking out at the kids playing in the back yard around the tree, with the

Christmas lights illuminating the scene, were some of the best memories that he had.

But slowly the joy leaked out. The marriage got unhappier. One Christmas near the end he decided to dress up as Santa Claus. He walked out on the street in front of the house, and Julia called the kids over to the window, and said "Look, look!" But Langley didn't want to think about that any more.

Something was bothering him, but he couldn't put his finger on it. It was like an empty thought bubble floating over his head. He knew he had to fill it with something—the right thing—before it popped. It could have been any number of things.

He had been fired from a job he loved. Well, that wasn't true. *Let's stop saying that now that you don't have to impress anyone,* he thought. *You never loved that job. You liked it well enough, but you did not love it.*

He had a brother who did not trust him and who actively campaigned against him. That would be enough to keep anyone awake at night. But Brian was not to blame wholly for that mess. Langley knew—*say it*—that he had fought against the landfill because it was his brother's client and he was—*say it*—jealous of his brother's continued success. The success Brian had at work, with his wife, with his children, in the community—Langley was jealous of his brother. Langley had never really been honest about that with himself. *Be honest, Langley, finally.*

His own family was three hundred miles away by land and a million miles away in thought. There again.

Langley smiled. *Quit it,* he said to himself, *or you might begin to think you're a bad person.*

On the application for his private investigator's license, in order to be approved according to the statute, he had to have demonstrated good moral character. It wasn't enough to say that this was true about himself. When he filled out the application, he had to very much believe it was true. He also had to prove on the application that there were no incidents of abuse toward his family and that he had met all his financial obligations to them. *Mental cruelty.* Those words popped into his head when he checked no on the question of abuse.

Financial obligations? He had met them up until Julia got married, but that was the minimum standard for any parent. You have to pay your way, but it is so much more than that. He had never been convicted of anything, and he had never "engaged in recklessness or negligence that endangered the safety of others."

As he scanned the public and private record of his life, he felt he could say honestly that he had fulfilled these obligations, but did that translate into having been a good person? Had he tried to do the right thing always? Isn't that what he had always been asked to do?

By definition he had passed the test, but he also knew of those incidents when he fell short, and he fell short spectacularly. These shortcomings seem to bleed out over the entire horizon of his life.

Ah, Langley, cut it out, he said again. He wanted to cut out all the white noise in his brain. He stood still for a few moments. There weren't even any crickets. The night was purple again. He went out to his small back yard and looked at the moon. It was just a tiny sliver, a fingernail, and the stars were sprinkled across the wide dark arm of the sky.

He did love his little town. He wanted to take a drive, to drive by Amsell's field to see it in the purple night. He wanted to see the blueberry bushes off Crow Road. He wanted to hear the peepers at the North Mill Pond. He wanted to walk up to Leonard's Hill, but he looked at his bottle of cabernet, and he had drunk about two-thirds of it.

Damn, he thought. *I'm not going anywhere.* Maybe that was what was bothering him most of all.

Twenty-One

Langley drove by Alfred Ramos's apartment the following day. The sky was a deep, reassuring blue, and Langley drove around the corner, parked the car, and walked to the end of the block and put seventy-five cents into an honor box for the morning *Union Leader.*

Langley was leaning against his car in what was not the best section of town. He painted a mental picture of the husband: a man who was pissed. Langley figured that the husband, booted out of his house, forced to do his own laundry, having to write his own checks for the heat, the electricity and the cable, was angry and he was going to make his wife pay. *It sucks,* thought Langley. *I know.*

He saw the front door of Ramos's apartment open, but he didn't look up. He simply folded the paper, opened his car door, got in and gave the guy a look. Ramos looked like he was scowling.

He followed Ramos to his job, which was at Manchester Hospital where he worked as an anesthesiologist. *OK,* Langley thought, *the guy is in the medical field. He would want to make sure his kid stayed healthy.* The guy looked OK to Langley. He didn't look tense or suspicious.

VIRGINIA AND RAMON WALKED to summer school together every morning except Wednesdays. Ramon was examined by the school nurse every morning, which was a request from the father and one the mother did not know about. They were checking to see if there were any bruises that had shown up on Ramon overnight or from over the weekend when the father had him. The reports, which were emailed to Lustig later on the same day, always came back completely clean.

"Well, we're committed to another week," said Lustig, archiving the email into the correct folder. He sighed. Another day was over. "What we're gonna do is go to my house, get some Chinese food delivered, have a few drinks, smoke a cigarette and relax."

"I'm happy to go out," said Langley, "if you don't want to eat at home. I always seem to be invading your house."

"I don't eat out," said Lustig. "What am I gonna do, be standing at the bar, say to some person I'm talking to, I'll be right back, I gotta go have a smoke? Have you ever seen those poor idiots outside a restaurant trying to have a cig? You think he's even enjoying it? Today, man, I'm all about comfort. If it isn't comfortable, I don't go do it. Simple as that."

He punched a number on his cell phone. "I'd like to order some food for delivery." Lustig ordered a smorgasbord of Chinese and Japanese food and gave only his name. Langley figured he ordered there all the time, and they knew who he was. "OK," said Lustig, picking up his keys. "If we leave now and go like a bat out of hell, we'll be there before the food."

LUSTIG'S EYES HAD THAT GREAT, glassy, faraway look that the eyes always have when too much bourbon has made its way into the bloodstream. He was blowing elegant smoke rings up toward the ceiling. Langley liked Lustig.

The guy was a man after his own heart. He smoked, he drank, he whistled. He had a compendium of bad and outdated habits that made him seem all too human and a character from another time.

They had been talking about the case, and Langley had been laying out his argument that somebody else besides the wife had injured the child, or that maybe it was a simple accident that had started this entire investigation. Langley said he believed that even the most acceptable and unpreventable accident involving the child was going to be used against the wife by the husband as evidence that she was hurting the child.

"Could be, could be," said Lustig, "but the kid was definitely banged up."

"You believe the husband," Langley said.

"I don't believe anybody. As far as I'm concerned, I hope that even if they both hate each other they leave the kid alone, that's what I hope. I hope no one is hurting anyone." He sighed. Lustig had had too much to drink. "We'll find out," he said aimlessly into the air. "One day, whether it's us or someone else, we'll find out."

Lustig struggled to get up off the couch. He was drunk, but he was also overweight, and when he was on his two feet he took off his tie and kicked off his shoes.

"Well," he said, "I gotta go to bed. You take the couch." It was after 2:00 a.m. "I've got to get a good night's sleep. I've got court first thing in the morning."

Twenty-Two

I hope no one is hurting anyone.

That's what Lustig had said last night, and with a pounding head, Langley opened his phone and pushed the number for his brother Brian.

They had not talked to each other in a month at least, but Langley didn't have anything to do. The Ramos child was in summer school, the mother was in the house, the father was at work, and so Langley had time to kill.

The law office's administrative assistant answered the phone. "Bessy and Calhoun."

"Yes, Brian Calhoun, please."

"Who may I say is calling?"

"His brother." Even though he had called this same number for years, the woman either was willfully forgetting the sound of his voice or had been told that he was not to be shown any courtesy.

Langley was certain—he was even hoping—that his call would go straight to voicemail. If that was so he could lie to himself and pretend he was the brother who at least tried to repair their relationship, but then Brian picked up.

"Langley," he said.

"Brian, how are you?"

"I'm, ah, I'm happy to hear from you."

"We don't have to take up too much time, but I figured I'd call and say hello." In fact, Langley's father had urged him repeatedly to keep talking to his brother, even if they were fighting.

"Thank you. How's it going?"

"Oh, you know, I'm just trying to get started, hang out my shingle, see what happens."

"You're good, though? Everything OK?"

"Yeah, you know, just doing my thing."

"Well, when the time is right, not now, but when the time is right, we'll make a plan for a cookout. The kids would be happy to see you. They miss you."

Langley, thinking like a younger brother, had the words *but you don't* pop into his head, but he didn't say anything.

"I'd love to see them."

"They're in Allentown now," Brian said, meaning they were visiting Langley's kids. "I can't ... they have to ... you know, they have to see their cousins."

"No, I know."

"I didn't know you knew."

"No," Langley said. "I didn't know they were in Allentown. What I meant was that I know that they have to see their cousins. It's important."

There was a pause.

"Listen," said Brian. "I don't know how you'd feel about this, but I may have some work for you, if you'd like. Maybe working for Bill Plano, which I know may not be palatable, but it could be lucrative. It's good work."

"I didn't think he thought I was very competent."

"Oh, knock it off," said Brian, and he said it so casually and amiably that he almost disarmed Langley. The two brothers shared a brief, airy laugh.

"Well, I'm glad you took my call," said Langley.

"Why wouldn't I?"
"Give everyone my love."
"No, you give everyone your love, OK?"
"You bet." Langley closed his phone slowly.

VIRGINIA RAMOS WAS IN LINE at the Home Depot about to check out with a Weber barbecue, six bags of charcoal briquettes, a three-pack of lighter fluid and a pack of wooden matches.

Langley stood behind her with a lamp that he did not need and did not want, but Virginia was with her son, and he wanted to hear the tone of her voice when she spoke to him. He wanted to analyze even the smallest gesture or to see if she said anything disparaging about the child to a clerk, a stranger, or even a friend if she happened to run into one.

But there wasn't anything. As she pushed her heavy cart away after she paid her bill, she glanced at Langley and gave him the briefest, most perfunctory of smiles. He realized that men must always be coming on to her. He probably looked to her like he was about to say something stupidly obvious, such as, "Someone's going to do a lot of grilling," which he actually was about to say when that perfectly studied, dismissive glance and smile were shot his way. He knew he had no reason to open his mouth.

He paid for his lamp. Virginia was strapping her child into the car seat when he walked by to get in his car. He was three parking spaces away, but when she leaned back out from buckling the belts and closed the door, she looked up again and saw Langley.

She smiled a little more warmly this time and said, "Beautiful day." She acknowledged him because she knew that was what most timid men wanted, just to be acknowledged, and then they would go away. Langley knew the routine.

"That it is," said Langley, happy that she had said something to him. That was as far as the exchange went. She got into her SUV just as Langley was getting into his car, and they both drove out of the Home Depot parking lot.

Langley had parked more than a half-mile away when he strolled up her block later that day. Somebody was grilling hamburgers. The whole street smelled like burgers. When he looked up, still more than a hundred feet from the house, he saw she was out on the front stoop talking on the phone. He couldn't walk by after seeing her today. That was no good. He started to turn around when he saw that Virginia looked in his direction. He slowly turned around. She went back into her house.

Goddamn, said Langley to himself. He wondered if she had seen his face. It had been stupid to go into Home Depot and get her attention. Bad judgment.

Twenty-Three

Selectmen's Chambers, Fenton Municipal Building Wednesday, Aug. 4, 7:00 p.m. The room was packed. Every chair was filled; more had been set up against the walls. There were people standing in the back. Maria Tull banged her gavel. *How she must love to do that,* thought Langley. The Town Council had called a public hearing on the proposal to build a Dirty Books franchise in Fenton on Route 136.

There was nothing specific that told Langley that any of this was related to the dead eagle, but he wanted to keep an eye on what his brother Brian and Bill Plano were doing. Brian was in the council chambers, of course, which was just as predictable as Plano's absence. Plano was a phantom who had his fingers in too many Fenton pies. *One day,* Langley thought to himself as he sat on his folding chair, *one day all this will come together.*

"Excuse me, people. The Deputy Fire Chief informs me that we are at capacity and can't accommodate anyone else," said Maria. There was still too much chatter in the air, and not enough people heard what Maria had said. She banged the gavel again. Maria was frowning.

"Please!" she said, and the room settled in to a low murmur. "We're going to keep the doors open because it will get hot in here, but we can't allow anyone else into the chambers. You'll just have to stay out in the hall."

There was a small roar when she said that, and someone yelled out, "Are you going to give everyone a chance to speak?"

"We've got until midnight and then we have to adjourn," she said. Langley turned around to see who she was talking to, but he couldn't see who it was.

"Can you make sure these people keep their presentation to a minimum, so we get a chance to speak?" the same person said. Langley didn't recognize the voice.

"We'll keep everything as ordered as we can, but we have to shut down at midnight," Maria said. "Those are the rules." There was more murmuring, and she banged the gavel again. "If you keep talking, we won't get started on time, and you'll have even less time for your part of the meeting," said Maria. That shut everyone up.

The news that Fenton had been chosen for the latest Dirty Books store franchise location had everyone buzzing. *The Fenton Herald* broke the story and followed it up with a series of articles about how inadequate the town's zoning laws had proved to be in preventing almost any kind of unwanted business from moving in. The paper editorialized about how that needed to change.

So the Board of Selectmen called a public hearing to let the owners of the so-called entertainment franchise make their case and allow town residents to have their say.

Langley noticed that Brian was sitting in the audience tonight. An outside attorney, Cindi Rush, was not from Brian's law firm. She was going to do most of the talking in front of the crowd.

That's a nice touch, thought Langley. *Have a woman come in and give the details of the pornographic video store. It'll turn it into a discussion on equality and civil rights, rather than a discussion on whether this is a suitable business for a place like Fenton.*

It was hot in the chambers, and people were fanning themselves with whatever they had to keep cool. Britney Sawuko was writing in her notebook. Cindi Rush, in a crisp business suit, stood in the front of the room next to a big flip chart. Langley noticed her calves. They bulged as if they were over-muscled. He looked at her and realized she probably didn't have an ounce of body fat on her.

This is a disciplined, smart person, thought Langley. She's *going to push this thing right through, if she can.*

"OK, all right," said Maria, looking around. "I'm going to promise an orderly meeting tonight. I don't want any outbursts. I want people to speak only at the public part of the meeting. If anybody tries to interrupt the attorneys, the traffic experts, or any of the members of the board here while they're talking, then I'll empty the room. I hope that's clear." Maria paused. "I know passions are running high. I know that. This is a sensitive subject. But we have to let everyone have their say." She looked around the room. "I know this is only the beginning of the discussion."

No one said anything. Maria introduced Cindi Rush. When the attorney stood, Langley made a bet with himself that the first thing she would do, the first thing anybody in this position does, would be to thank the community for taking an interest in what happens in their own town.

"I want to thank everyone for coming out tonight," said Cindi Rush, and Langley smiled. He had been to hundreds and hundreds of these meetings. "I know this is important to you, to your town and to your families." She paced. "I want to dispel a few notions that have made their way into print and into the public discussion. There are always,

always intimations about criminal elements being associated with the ownership of a business such as this. Let me first say that this is a business owned by a consortium of businesspeople who are family people such as yourselves." Here Langley wondered if Cindi Rush wasn't going to overextend herself right off the bat, because the crowd started to stir. "They are not in the Mafia, they are not part of a criminal enterprise. Not one of you here may choose to go into this sort of business, and I understand that, but adult entertainment, if you're not familiar with it, has come a long way from your memories of when it first emerged into the public eye forty years ago. The companies who manufacture this entertainment are legitimate, healthy, publicly owned and privately held corporations."

She walked slowly in front of the selectmen's dais. "Let me ask you a question. How many of you people here tonight would hesitate to do business with a Marriott? Or a Holiday Inn? Or the Sheraton? Have you all stayed there at one time or another with your families? Your children? I think all of you would, and probably have, and I want to remind you that each of these corporations offer, in the privacy of their hotel rooms, the products that this franchise will be providing at their new location. These hotels are respectable, even iconic, American institutions, dedicated to providing the safest and most comfortable accommodations anywhere you go across our beautiful country. They wouldn't be in business if they didn't."

She paused. Langley looked intently at Maria Tull's face. He was trying to read her, but she was inscrutable. Langley also knew that Cindi Rush had scored one for the away team. Langley craned his neck slightly to see Brian, who was sitting with his legs crossed, taking notes.

"This franchise is one of the safest businesses you can have in your town. There are twenty-six franchise locations across New England, and I will tell you exactly how many police or fire calls have been made to these locations in the past three years. None. Zero. Twenty-six locations in six New England states and not one problem. If you compare these stats to how many police calls, injuries and deaths there have been associated with bars, a perfectly legal and honorable business, across New England in that same period, the difference is, as you can imagine, staggering."

Langley looked around the room. He saw Freddie Ouillette, who owned a bar, and Langley wondered how Freddie was reacting to that last statement.

Cindi Rush introduced an architect who went through the aesthetics of the rather modest structure. With her artist renderings, the architect demonstrated how there would be easy access in and out of the parking lot. She showed how the front of the building would be tastefully landscaped. She talked about how many cars the parking lot would hold. She mentioned the hours of operation and that the store would be closed on national holidays. She said the sign would be far smaller than town zoning laws allowed.

Langley noticed how each of the speakers took pains not to mention the actual name of the store. It was "the business," "the franchise," "the location," or anything else other than Dirty Books.

The traffic expert said, as they always do, that even though there would be a new business in the neighborhood, there would be no impact to the traffic patterns along Route 136. None at all. It would be as though the new business wasn't even there.

Cindi Rush finished her portion of the agenda. She reminded the good citizens of Fenton that this business was planned for a site along Route 136 that was zoned for business. It was not even a restricted use business zone, and there was nothing in the town's ordinances that prevented a new business with an adult theme from opening in that part of town.

"I just want to remind you that this is legal and acceptable. This company will be an excellent corporate citizen, adding to the town's tax base, offering legal employment to those who want it," Rush said. "We know how important quality of life is to the citizens of Fenton."

"No you don't," someone shouted out.

Maria grimaced and banged her gavel. "Ed?" she said. "Eddie Griffin, you keep your mouth shut," and everybody laughed.

"We do. We honestly do, and we will honor that," said Cindi Rush. "I guarantee you. In just a few short months you will drive down Route 136 and not even notice the store is there." Langley smiled. She was probably right about that.

Maria Tull looked at her watch. "It's almost nine o'clock. Does anybody want to take a bio-break?" This was Maria's term for giving people time to go to the bathroom. There was some assent from the crowd that a short break wouldn't be a bad thing.

"OK, we're going to take a break for ten minutes." She banged the gavel, and the crowd dispersed. "And I mean ten minutes. Those of you who smoke can go and smoke."

Langley stayed in his seat and watched Brian walk up to Cindi Rush. He could tell that Brian was congratulating her on a job well done. She smiled and shook her head and gestured in such a way that she felt she had gotten her point across. Langley closed his notebook and closed his eyes.

"So, how do you like them Dirty Books?" It was Amy Hargreaves, with whom Langley had gone to high school. He opened his eyes with a start.

"I doubt they have anything I don't already own," Langley said.

"Me either. How are you, Chief?" She sat in a seat in the row behind him.

"I'm good. How's the family? Frank, everybody?"

"They're good. He's at Fenway tonight with the kids, thank God. Me and Alicia—do you know Alicia?" Langley shook his head that he didn't. "We're going out to the Foreside after this and have a few drinks if you want to come along."

"That sounds great, thanks."

"Everything good with you?"

"Yeah, I mean, it's been an adjustment. I was a little surprised at how things turned out, job-wise."

"Well, Maria Tull's a bitch." Amy said it without malice or any real feeling at all. She and Langley laughed a little. "OK, we'll see you later on, maybe. Alicia's nice." She winked and patted Langley on the shoulder and left.

The crowd filed back in, murmuring, and everyone settled in their seats or stood in the places they had chosen for themselves. There was about half of the original crowd left. Maria banged the gavel. "We're going to start the public part of the agenda. This is going to go like this. If someone wants to speak, I want you to go to the microphone, state your name and your address clearly. This is not the time for making public speeches, although some of you undoubtedly will." The crowd laughed lightly. "This is a time for questions for the attorneys, for the experts. Keep your question brief, and we'll be able to get more of you in. OK. People are beginning to line up already. State your name, sir."

"Jason Santini, 73 Meadow Brook Lane, Fenton. I just want to ask Miss Rush if she would want a business like this in her town?"

Langley shook his head. This was a bad way to start off. He pinched the bridge of his nose and squeezed his eyes shut.

Cindi Rush stood. "Mr. Santini, I live in Salmon Falls, less than twenty miles from here, where one of the largest locations of this franchise is located. I have one in my town, and I have two children."

The next woman said, "Miss Rush, what is the name of the store that is being proposed along Route 136?"

"It's called Dirty Books."

"Good," said the woman. "I just wanted to hear you actually say it." The crowd laughed and clapped. Cindi Rush gave the tiniest shrug of her shoulders, as if to say, "Is this the best you've got?"

Antonio Meli moved up to the microphone and stated his name and address. "I'd like to ask Mr. Brian Calhoun, sitting so quietly over there, a question, if I may?"

Brian turned around. He didn't say anything.

"Who actually owns this franchise, Brian, can you tell us that?"

Maria banged her gavel. "Mr. Meli, you'll address either the Chairman or one of the scheduled speakers."

"Who do we call if we have a complaint? Bill Plano? He's one of the owners of Spiral Enterprises, isn't he?"

Maria kept banging her gavel, and people started to applaud.

"And I'd just like to know if Mr. Calhoun's law firm is dedicated to turning all of Route 136, or all of Fenton, into a cesspool. We have a landfill there now—clean, my ass." The crowd erupted. "And now this. Where is Bill Plano anyway? Why can't we talk directly to him?"

Maria was banging her gavel.

"What's next, Brian? Strip clubs? Strip malls?" The crowd was cheering and clapping, but Brian did not acknowledge the commotion.

Maria kept banging her gavel, and she motioned to one of the cops, Officer Ruggerio, who walked over to Antonio. "Mr. Meli, please," said the officer, taking hold of Antonio's elbow. This was a good cop, Langley thought.

"Fenton, New Hampshire, is not some place you can just turn into whatever you want," said Antonio. Officer Ruggerio took hold of his arm a little more firmly, but Antonio broke free.

"Even if the law does allow it, how can something happen here if the people don't want it? The crowd cheered. "How can that happen?"

Officer Ruggerio led Antonio out of the building. He would just tell him to go home. Maria kept banging her gavel over and over, and the crowd, buzzing and laughing, eventually settled down.

It became very quiet. Brian kept taking notes, as though he didn't care, but Langley knew how Brian felt about that old man.

Maria looked around the room. "We are a nation of laws," she said. "You people should know that."

"The law isn't always right," someone yelled. The crowd clapped, and Maria resumed banging her gavel until everyone settled down.

"What are our options here?" said Arthur Kumin, standing at the microphone. "I guess this is for the attorney and for the board. What options do we really have to keep this business out of the town? I've been to Salmon Falls and seen the store over there. I urge everyone to go. It's disgusting."

"What did you find disgusting about it?" said Cindi Rush, moving again to the front of the crowd.

"It's just a disgusting place."

"I understand you have an opinion about the ..."

"Have you ever been inside that place?"

"I have," said Rush, matter-of-factly.

"What did you think about it?"

"Mister ... ?"

"Kumin. Dr. Kumin."

"I'm asking you a very specific question. What is specifically disgusting about the physical look of the, of the ... Dirty Books store in Salmon Falls?" The crowd laughed lightly.

"Well, you know what goes on in there."

"I'm not asking you that, Dr. Kumin."

Langley looked over at Brian, and he saw Brian gesture with his hand, ever so slightly, asking Cindi Rush to tone it down just a little bit. Just a bit.

"What I don't want," said Cindi Rush in a slightly nicer voice, "Is for people to project too many of their opinions about the products sold inside the store to the look of the building. Dr. Kumin, I understand your unhappiness, but if you took down the sign in front of the store in Salmon Falls, the truth is you wouldn't have any idea what was sold inside. Not a clue."

Langley looked over and saw Brian nodding his head slightly.

"You won't have to live with it," said someone in the crowd.

"If you have something to say, please say it on the record and into the microphone," said Maria.

Jonah King, the man who had just spoken, started to make his way to the microphone. He was going to move to the front of the line.

"Not now, Jonah, you have to wait your turn," said Maria, and the crowd laughed.

"Jonah can go ahead," said the woman in front of the microphone.

"Jonah King, 232 Irving Road, Fenton. Thank you. I just wanted to say that out-of-town lawyers who come to a place like Fenton and ... and they change our way of life and then they leave and they don't have to deal with the effects of their decisions. We're left to pick up the pieces."

The audience applauded.

"Well, Mr. King, as I said, I live in Salmon Falls and I have children," said Cindi. "You know Brian Calhoun, who lives here, and he has two children." There were scattered boos, which surprised Langley and certainly surprised Brian. "And while obviously there is opposition to the business, as shown here in this room, I can assure you not everyone in Fenton is opposed to it."

"I would like to go back to Dr. Kumin's original question," said a shy-looking woman who was barely tall enough to speak into the microphone.

"State your name," said Maria, and everybody laughed because it was Maria's own daughter Deidre.

"Deidre Tull," she said, and everyone laughed again. "22 Margeson Way." She lived at home with her mother. "I would also like to know what we can actually do to keep this business out of town."

Eb Webb, the town's attorney, stood. "I'm Eb Webb, attorney for the town of Fenton, and after reading our zoning laws and consulting with the Zoning Board, our zoning ordinances accommodate this kind of business."

"Then there isn't much we can do to stop it," Deidre Tull asked.

"If you don't want any more businesses like this in your town," said Cindi, "then you'll have to change your ordinances, but this one should be allowed in."

The laws would eventually be changed, which suited the owners of the Dirty Books store just fine. After they opened their shop, they'd be the only game in town. The whole thing made Langley want to crack that little town—and his brother—wide open.

Twenty-Four

It was the following night when Virginia Ramos stood in the middle of her living room screaming into the phone. Ramon had gone to bed, and Virginia was not holding back. Langley was in the yard next door, precariously hidden, feeling anxious, but he wanted to hear what was being said. Her windows were open.

Virginia spoke some Spanish, which he had not heard her speak before, and she spoke loudly, harshly, and then she ended the call. She paced back and forth with her arms crossed and the phone still in her hand. It rang again, and Virginia answered and shouted, "No!"

The phone rang again and she yelled, "Stop!" and hung up again. The phone rang a third time and Virginia threw the phone into the couch. She sat herself down on the couch and crossed her arms. She picked up the phone and looked at it.

Langley walked across the street and down the block and got into his rental car to wait. He sat there for a little more than a half-hour and simply watched. A car came down the street. The car parked in front of Virginia's house, and Langley was certain that it was Alfred Ramos' car. Ramos got out of the car, and he was carrying an oblong object in his hands that looked like a rifle.

"Oh, shit," said Langley, opening his car door and getting out. He started walking to the house as he watched

Ramos walk up to the front door and pound on it. When Virginia opened the door, he punched his way in.

"Fuck," said Langley. He started to run, and he could hear screaming. He dialed 911 as he was running across the neighboring lawns. He told the dispatcher he thought he was witnessing a domestic dispute and gave the address.

Just as he was finishing the call, Langley heard a gunshot. He took his gun out of his holster and ran into the house.

He pushed through the open door and aimed his firearm at Ramos, who was half-crouched on the floor with his hands covering his face. Virginia was standing over him with a gun in her hand. There was a bullet hole in the wall right above Ramos's head. Langley smelled gunpowder. Either she wanted to miss, or she was a bad shot, but this was not what Langley expected.

"Please!" shouted Ramos, cowering on his knees.

Virginia was trembling. Her eyes were dark, furious. She began pointing her gun alternately at Ramos and Langley. Her arms were shaking. She looked wildly at Langley. "Who are you, who are you, who are you?" she repeated.

"He works for me!" Ramos shouted from his crouched position.

"What?" Virginia said.

"Please stay calm," Langley said.

"Why are you here?" She was shrieking. Langley could hear the sirens. *Please, God,* he said, *hurry up.*

"You think I'm going to hand my son over to him? That monster? That piece of shit?!"

That's when Langley noticed Ramos had a box of toy golf clubs at his feet.

"Who do you think is going to take care of my child when I'm gone?" Her voice was the wildest human voice that Langley had ever heard. "He's trying to run me down!"

The police cars were pulling up the street. They were almost here. Virginia aimed her gun at Ramos, pulled the trigger, and hit him in the neck. Blood spurted out as he wrapped his fingers around the exploded skin, and he was choking.

Their seven-year-old boy came walking into the room, a silent witness.

Virginia aimed her gun at Langley and fired, and then, Langley later learned, she turned the gun on herself.

Twenty-Five

The first person Langley saw when he opened his eyes was his ex-wife Julia. When he saw her he thought that things must really be bad.

The first conscious thing he did was to try to wiggle his toes. He could. He then wiggled his fingers. He could. He wasn't paralyzed. He was able to believe vaguely that if he was not paralyzed, then he might have gotten off lucky, but he was still unsure exactly what damage had been done.

The first words he said to his ex-wife were, "I'm going to need a good chiropractor."

It was the kind of thing he would have said in the old days, and she laughed. His two girls, Patty and Annie, hugged him, and in the wavy horizon of his vision he saw his father. He was alive. Before he closed his eyes again, he thought he had seen Delia Reed leaving the room. Then he blacked out.

Virginia Ramos had done some damage. The bullet tore through the upper part of his right shoulder. It had shattered his collar bone and ripped out some of the cords of his neck muscle. She had missed an artery by a paper thin margin.

A lot of blood had drained out of him, but he was lucky that the police had arrived—were practically in the house—when he was shot. He had a nine-hour surgery to put everything back together again, and he was wired up and dripped up. His entire body was under surveillance.

Langley drifted in and out of consciousness. Through his open eyes he saw his father and his brother Brian and Brian's wife Eileen and their children. He saw his father's new girlfriend Vance, and he saw some of his colleagues from the force. But everything seemed to be silent, wordless. Cards from cops from all over the country started to appear. Langley wondered in his stupor how news could travel so fast. He was visited by the new chief of police. Antonio Meli came by. Lustig dropped by.

Langley remembered holding out his hands and speaking slurred words with lopsided smiles. Some strangers drifted in and out. He seemed to see them only for a few seconds as his eyes fluttered open and shut.

He never really knew how long he was conscious, or unconscious. Every time he opened his eyes someone new seemed to be in the room. Hours passed, perhaps days. He didn't know. He never knew.

The doctors, the nurses, the nursing aides, the cleaning people, they all came and went. Slowly, he was conscious long enough to listen to conversations. *How are you feeling? Is there anything you need? Is there any pain? Can you feel that? Can you hear this?*

And slowly, slowly, Langley started to respond verbally.

"I feel like shit."

"I need to get out of the hospital."

"There is pain everywhere."

Brian came by almost every day. He stood awkwardly around Langley's bed. Eileen came by every night to give him a hug.

As Langley began to recover, as he was able to sit up and read the cards and letters and to talk to the doctors about his prognosis, he also became angry. He felt resentment toward his town and about what had happened. He felt a surging anger toward his brother. Langley felt that Brian probably went home every night and justified everything that had happened.

"I have to do what's right for me and my family," Langley could hear in his thoughts, "I had no idea it would come to this." He would argue in his lawyerly way that "Langley is his own worst enemy, you know."

Langley right then did not feel warm or grateful toward his brother when he came to visit. His rage at Brian was mixed up with his rage at Virginia Ramos, at his pain, at having to take that ridiculous job because he was ousted as police chief.

"This never would have happened if I had been able to stay in Fenton," said Langley through clenched teeth. He was talking to Delia.

"Sshhh, sshhh." She ran her hands through his hair over and over again, just running her hands over his head. Tears spilled from her eyes. "You can be angry later, but please don't be angry now," she said. She blinked her eyes, and her tears fell down onto Langley's sheets. "Just stay quiet and get better, and you'll be able to deal with all of this when you get out."

"Where are Julia and the kids?" he asked.

"They've gone home," said Delia. She told him to be quiet again. "I'm sorry I'm crying," she said, blowing her nose, and then she really started to sob. She ran her hands through his hair again. "I'll come back in a little while," she said, "I'll be back in a little while."

Then Brian came in. He had brought the newspaper and some magazines. Langley sort of waved him off. He didn't want to speak to anyone. He didn't want to see his brother. Langley was weak, but he was also in a foul mood. He wanted to get out of the hospital. Brian moved a chair up next to Langley's bed.

What is this about, Langley thought to himself. *What's Brian thinking about?* Eileen came in with fresh flowers.

Brian put his hand into Langley's to hold it. Langley grasped Brian's hand. The medication he was taking made him woozy, and he wasn't really able to speak. He had an infection. Langley was angry at all of it. So when Brian took Langley's hand, Langley tightened his grip. He squeezed.

Brian wasn't sure what to do. "We'll talk when you're feeling better," he said softly. He stood and tried to get free without Eileen noticing. He pulled at Langley's hand. Langley, with his torso on fire, with his neck and face burning up, didn't let go. "OK, OK," said Brian, a tight smile forming on his face.

But Langley held on.

"Langley," said Brian, his voice still quiet but filled with frustration and anger. Langley knew that Brian was trying to stay calm as he tried to pry his brother's fingers loose.

Langley, tears squeezing out of the corners of his eyes, fixed his fierce stare on Brian's face.

"We have to go." Brian was sweating. He was trying to pull away. Eileen stood there watching. Then she slowly walked up to the bed and folded both her hands over Langley's and Brian's intertwined hands. Langley held tight. Brian looked at his wife. She gently spread their fingers open and finally set them apart.

Brian flexed his fingers. Stepping back, he gave Langley a defiant look.

"Go right ahead," said Langley in his garbled voice. "I don't care anymore."

Twenty-Six

When members of the Manchester Police Department and the New Hampshire State Police visited Langley in his hospital room, it was more of a perfunctory Q & A than a probe as to what actually happened. When they arrived, they were accompanied by Ed Lustig. Chloe Brooke, Langley's attorney, was already in the room.

The Manchester cops didn't know how Langley fit into the thing when they first came through Virginia Ramos's door the night he was shot. He was bleeding, lying on the floor conscious, he had his gun out, and the cops at first, not unreasonably, figured that Langley had shot both of them. He still had his gun in his hand as he lay on the floor bleeding.

Phone records showed that Langley was the one who dialed 911, and Lustig, of course, confirmed that Langley was working for him. Ballistics later confirmed that all the bullets that had been fired that night—the one in Langley's shoulder, the two that killed Alfred Ramos and Virginia Ramos, and the slug in the wall—had come from the gun that had Virginia Ramos's fingerprints on it.

It turned out, though, that Langley had been right about what was happening in the Ramos family. The State Police and the staff at the state's Health and Human Services Division believed that Alfred Ramos had been physically abusing the child and psychologically abusing his wife all along.

"He was making her paranoid for years, blaming her for every cough, every illness, every bruise, everything and anything," said the state cop, a woman by the name of Van Dine. "He pushed her to the edge."

"Over the edge," said Langley.

"He was gaslighting her for years," said Lustig. "Poor thing."

"How is the boy?" asked Langley.

"He's fine. He's in a foster home," said Lustig. "Everyone is trying to do their best to figure out how much trauma he's suffered ..." Lustig's voice trailed off. He seemed truly saddened. "Maybe he doesn't really know what happened."

"He's got to know that his parents aren't around anymore," Langley said. "He's got to know. He can't not know. You know when someone is dead."

Twenty-Seven

When the bandages came off his right shoulder, that section of his body looked like it had been grafted onto his body. He was standing in front of the mirror in his hospital room. The spot where the bullet exploded was a hideous map of stitches and cuts and purple bruises. He gently traced the stitches up into his neck, and then he paused to feel his pulse. He listened to the pumping in his veins. The rhythm was steady and hard and tense.

When he tried to move his right arm, ever so gently, his body responded violently. "Goddamn," he said.

"Well, Kojak, how are you feeling?" His father's question was genuine, and Langley was even touched by the antiquated cultural reference. His father was holding his hand. Langley couldn't remember him ever doing that before. "I cleared everyone out of this room. I wanted some time with my son."

Langley smiled. He didn't cry because if he cried, it would hurt like a bastard. "I actually feel pretty good," he said in a voice that still sounded unlike his own.

"So," said the old man, "Who told you that you were cut out to be a private eye?"

"What have the doctors told you, because I know you've asked?"

"That you're going to lose mobility in your left arm. You won't be able to lift it up. A John McCain kind of deal." John McCain was the old man's hero. "You'll look a little awkward."

"I can deal with that."

"You're going to have some pain."

"Really?"

The old man put his head down and smiled. "They're going to ... they're going to ...."

Langley looked at his father, who put his head into the crook of Langley's arm. He was crying. The tough old man was sobbing.

Langley carefully put his hand on his father's head. His dad didn't even try to stop crying. He just let it all out, let it go, and when he lifted his head he didn't say the usual thing, which was to say he was sorry for making a spectacle of himself. It didn't matter. The old man had had a heart attack not so long ago, his son had been almost murdered, his two boys were estranged, his beloved wife was gone too soon, another son was dead, and because of all that, there was no longer any time left to hide his feelings. Everything was too far gone to be reticent about the depth of the love he felt for his children.

And so the old man started to tell Langley some things. He said he especially felt something unique toward Langley. Langley always seemed a step or two behind Brian, the old man said. Langley was good, even great, but Brian seemed to be, or seemed to act, that much better. He knew Langley was damaged, and he knew why, his father said.

His father wanted to apologize for something. When Langley was a kid his father, for a brief period of time, called Brian "Fred" and Langley "Gene." It was his joke, and he was referencing Fred Astaire and Gene Kelly. He did that because as great as Gene Kelly was, he was always that much behind Astaire. His father always thought that Langley was that much behind Brian.

He had thought it would push Langley to do better, but it made the boy withdraw, and in the softness of his approaching old age, the old man knew that it had been a mistake. "You should never do that to a child," he said to Langley. "I'm sorry," he said over and over. "I'm sorry."

One of the last things his wife had told him before she died was to forgive himself for anything he felt he had done to the boys, and so he was trying to do that.

AFTER HIS FATHER HAD GONE HOME, Langley lay on his bed with its hideous rubber covering beneath the sheets and stared at the ceiling. He turned off the TV. He heard people mumbling out in the hallway. His door was open. He saw an old man walk down the corridor with an aide helping him. The man's hands were shaking. He saw various nurses and doctors walking by his door, everyone on a mission, none of it very pleasant. He wanted to get the hell out of this place. He was thinking about what his father had said.

He put his hands over his eyes and started to cry. It was time to clean up so many things. It was time to confront some things. He would quit working for Ed Lustig for a while. He would go back to Fenton. He would try to ask Delia out on a date. And he would start asking about that eagle again.

Something about the sight of that eagle lying in the bed of dried leaves, something about the violence that had been done to it, made it stick in his head. Yes, he would go home and try to figure it all out.

THE DAY LANGLEY WAS DISCHARGED from the hospital he sat for two hours in a wheelchair waiting for someone called a hospitalist to come by and finish the necessary paperwork so he could go home. He was promised several times that someone would come by and let him out.

With him on that day were his father, and Vance, and Delia Reed. Just those three. They all sat around anxiously. No one was talking because they knew that Langley had had enough of the hospital, had had enough of not feeling well.

Finally, his father stood and said, "Let's go."

BOOK TWO

Twenty-Eight

Langley was sitting in Delia's apartment. He was sitting on the couch and looking at the bookshelves and the prints and paintings on the walls and the color of her furniture, and he was listening to the music she was playing, which was soft jazz. Not the kind of music Langley would have played, but it fit the mood of the apartment perfectly.

Delia had coffee table books on plants and birds and wildlife. The prints on the walls showed flowers and paintings of old New England harbors filled with ships and New England towns dominated by a single white spire of the local church. A Persian rug covered the floor, and a beautifully marked tiger cat crouched on the back of a chair taking the scene in. The cat was named Scout.

It fits, Langley thought, *that Delia is a cat person: they are independent. What's the old saying? Cats don't have owners, they have staff.*

The walls were painted a soft white, an off-white almost cream color, a color right out of the natural world. The color of lilies. There were green plants in the corners of the apartment. Langley thought the way that Delia had decorated the place reflected her personality almost exactly.

You could be standing there, never having met Delia in your life, and when she came walking around the corner, incredibly trim and fit and smiling and unworried, you would simply say, ah, yes, that's the person who lives here. That's what Langley thought.

He knew his own house looked like something out of a David Lynch movie. It was like the creepy living rooms in *Blue Velvet,* angular, dim, with colorless chairs and dull walls. Rooms with an unlived-in, industrial feel to them. Maybe that was his personality. He didn't think it was, but maybe that was what he had become.

"So you were a cop, eh?" Langley was talking to Zamira Berenfield, Delia's friend. He had been happy to have been invited by Delia to come to dinner. But not long after he arrived, he heard words he thought were just as fatal as, "I only like you as a friend." When he came through the door Delia said, "Oh, I also invited over another friend, if you don't mind."

Langley did mind. He wasn't happy. So he balanced a glass of wine on his knees, and Delia made dinner in the kitchen. Zamira asked about his life as a cop. The last thing he wanted to do was talk about that. The only thing he wanted to talk about less than any of those other things was how he got shot.

"Tell Z how you got shot," said Delia from the kitchen.

"Oh, my God, that's right, you were shot," said Zamira, and she seemed genuinely shocked and hurt by the thought of such violence. But she also seemed impressed.

"Just like Fitty Cent," said Langley, employing the same kind of outdated cultural reference his father would use.

Zamira laughed a little but then abruptly stopped and said, "No, really, what happened?"

Langley often told the story of How I Got Shot. He had told it at supermarkets, at restaurants. He told it to newly minted police cadets. Every time he told it his arm seemed to flare up, and it was one side effect of the event that did not thrill him. But he did find that the more he told the story, the less he dreamed about it, so perhaps it was a good thing.

Zamira was a small, lovely woman. She seemed about thirty-five and had long, black hair. He enjoyed talking to her and looking at her. He wondered if Delia had asked him over to not only cheer him up but to set him up on a date.

"Your family must have been devastated," said Zamira.

"My father was going through hell. I think he was beside himself. He had just had a heart attack, so I was worried, too. He was tense."

"Do you have any brothers and sisters?"

"He has a brother who's an asshole," said Delia.

He's not an asshole, thought Langley, but he didn't say it out loud. This was also a question Langley hated because he never knew how to answer it. "Yes, I have a brother," he said quietly.

Zamira shot Delia a glance as though she knew there was more to the story than that.

"Tell her about your other brother," said Delia. "Please," she said. "I want to hear about him, too."

Langley sighed.

"Langley had a brother who died," said Delia.

"I'm so sorry," said Zamira. She reached out and touched Langley on the arm.

Langley got up to get more wine. He wanted a cigarette. "I have a brother named Brian, and we had a brother who was Brian's twin," said Langley.

He saw Delia mouth, "He never talks about it," to Zamira. He was thinking of his mother and father, and he was thinking about Brian.

"What happened? Was he sick?" asked Zamira.

"No, no," said Langley. He sighed. He closed his eyes, he grimaced. He rocked back on his heels. He let out his breath with the words, "He fell out of a tree."

At the moment he said those words, he saw himself reaching up to his older brother Danny, Brian's twin, so Danny could hoist Langley farther up this big old bull pine that Danny had climbed. They were already about halfway up, just the two of them. When he grabbed Danny's hand, Langley joked a bit and tugged on it. The next thing he knew Danny fell below him onto a branch. The branch snapped, and the sharp nub of the broken branch ripped a gash the length of Danny's rib cage, tearing him open.

Danny dropped to the lawn. Langley fell after him. Danny lay crumpled up with his guts pumping out of him. Danny was screaming, and then he whimpered and fell silent. He looked like a sliced open animal.

Langley ran inside to shout for his parents. When they got out to the tree, Danny, who was twelve, was dead. As they left for the hospital that night, shell-shocked, Brian walked up to Langley and smashed him in the mouth.

"Langley? Langley?" Delia was standing next to him, and when he looked up, she hugged him and kissed him on the cheek so tenderly that Langley impulsively hugged her. The moment seemed so intimate that Zamira actually looked away.

"I don't think I can tell that story," said Langley.

"You don't have to," said Delia.

Zamira left not long after, and Delia sat close to him on the couch, his hand in hers. "I'm sorry I brought it up," she said.

"It's not that. I just that after I was shot, I thought my father was going to lose two kids, and that just seemed so ... unfair." But that wasn't it, of course. How do you talk about the death of a brother, a death that you think is your fault?

Delia smiled. "Well," she said, "Do you ...?" and Langley thought maybe she was going to ask him to spend the night. But she sighed and said, "Do you want some more wine?" She poured him a glass, and they sat on the couch for a while. Suddenly she asked, "What are you going to do next? Do some more work for that lawyer?"

"I guess so. I don't have anything else to do. Or I could do nothing. I'm a man of independent means, as they say."

"You are?"

"No, I'm kidding."

"Oh, well, geez, you got my hopes up." She was rubbing his shoulder.

"I have my pension. I suppose I could become the head of security at some mall or something."

"You could handle those teenaged shoplifters."

"There wouldn't be any teenaged shoplifters, not with Langley on the case," he joked.

Delia laughed lightly and looked at Langley. Langley looked at her. He liked her face. He liked her eyes, he liked her smile.

"I think I'm going to find out what happened to that eagle," said Langley.

"Why, um, what made you think of that?"

"I don't know," Langley said, but he did know. He did know. “It's going to bring up all that shit again with my brother."

"I think knowing maybe will tie up a lot of loose ends for you," said Delia. The way she said it made Langley think she knew more about him than she let on. "I don't mean that the way it sounded," she said, blushing.

"No, I want to know," Langley said. He never could stand the fact that the bird had been killed right under his nose and Antonio had never gotten any satisfaction about what had happened.

"You're not hampered by being employed by the town. You don't have to worry about upsetting the tax base," she said, and she smiled when she said that.

"Right, right," said Langley.

"Anyway, I can guarantee you that at some point, at some time in your life, you're going to stop and think, I wonder what the hell ever happened to that bird?"

Twenty-Nine

By mid-October his arm had healed nicely. There were no more infections. He took his meds just as he was told. Delia was offering him some alternative ways to heal his body. He was not quite ready for yoga, he told her, but he was doing his best to follow her suggestions. He drank her special tea, even though he thought it tasted like wheat.

He looked at his lopsided figure in the mirror, and he was still pissed.

The answer to his question, what would make a person kill another, was on his mind when Ed Lustig came by to give Langley his check.

"I docked you the last day you didn't work, you know, the day you were supposed to work after you got shot and all," Lustig said as he made himself comfortable on Langley's couch. He laughed at his own joke. "Jesus Christ," he added, feeling the cushions he was sitting on. "Take some of that cash and buy yourself a new couch. Where did you buy this, at the quarry?"

Lustig got up and made his way over to a chair. He sat, stretched his legs, and crossed them. He took out a cigarette and made a gesture toward Langley to ask if it was OK to smoke.

"Ed, I gotta tell ya, I'd rather you not. I haven't had one since I got shot."

"I won't say you're better off," said Lustig as he put the cigarette behind his ear. He took an envelope out of his inside jacket pocket and put it on the table. "Three grand," he said. Langley nodded. "Did you read the report?"

"I did," Langley said.

"This was one fucked-up family, never should have had kids." Lustig was up and walking around. Not smoking was making him nervous. He was looking at the walls, which no doubt felt like they were closing in.

Langley said, "Ed, if you want to smoke ..."

"No, no," he waved him off. "You're my inspiration."

"I want to tell you something," said Langley.

Lustig raised a brow. "Should I commit myself to being your attorney now so I won't have to divulge anything you tell me?"

"It's nothing like that."

"Do you think you screwed up in some way?"

"Let me just tell you."

"OK." Ed took the cigarette out from behind his ear and lit it. "I'm sorry," he said. "You're making me nervous."

"When I first saw the husband, even though you had told me his name was Ramos, when I first saw him ..." Langley took a deep breath.

"You felt just a twinge of prejudice."

"Yes, right."

"Had all those stereotypes of Latinos running around in your head. Violence. Gangs. Things like that."

"Yes."

"It didn't matter that the guy was educated, had a good job, was esteemed by his colleagues."

"I just, I just ..."

"Never mind, you just. The guy happened to be nuts," said Lustig. "Didn't matter what color his skin was, what he did. His culture had nothing to do with it." He sighed.

"People who never get out of the house are the only ones who can afford their own prejudices, you know that?"

"I know."

"You know," said Lustig. "You don't know. You should see what walks through my door." He puffed for a moment. "The other problem, though," said Lustig.

"Which is what?"

"That you felt, um, protective of the wife?"

"Yes."

"It turns out you should have been. So? What's your confession? That you came face to face with a demon you didn't think you had? You're not colorblind?"

"I think so."

"Welcome to the big club," said Lustig. "At least you're admitting it." He smoked for a second and asked, "Do you think your professional behavior was influenced by the way you felt?"

"Once, yes," said Langley.

Lustig took a deep breath.

"I, uh, I followed Virginia Ramos into the Home Depot in Manchester, and I think I told myself that I needed to, that it was necessary, and when I was behind her in line . . . "

"You were that close?"

"She looked at me and nodded."

"OK."

"And when I ran into the house the night of the shooting, she clearly recognized me. She asked over and over again who I was."

"This was after she shot at the husband?"

"Yes."

"But before she killed him?"

"Yes."

"She was confused."

"I think so."

"So what would you like me to say?"

"Is it possible ... "

"Is it possible that her recognition of you ratcheted up her anxiety enough to shoot her husband when you think she might not have?"

"I wonder."

"How do you know she recognized you?"

"Well, the way she was asking me, I assumed so."

"You assumed. What were her words when you got in the house? Who are you?"

"That's right, but she was asking because she had seen me before."

"You have too much information in your head. She would have said the same thing to anyone who entered her house after she fired a shot. You could have been someone walking up the street. Who are you? You were carrying a gun. Wouldn't you ask the same thing? She probably thought you were there to protect the husband."

"I think ..."

"I'm going to do you a favor. I'm going to save you thousands of dollars in therapy. The only thing that happened that night that was not going to happen at some point was you getting shot." Lustig was hot. He was mad. "You, who thought the husband was coming in with a gun to hurt the woman you had so privately fallen in love with."

Langley was embarrassed that Ed Lustig had read him so easily.

"You're just a bit player in this drama. Virginia Ramos had a gun, it was loaded. She had gone out and bought it, and she fired it almost as soon as her husband walked in the door. Even before you had shown up."

"That's true."

"She missed the first time. You walk in so she can shoot him and you, and then she kills herself. That's all. The way I look at it, honestly, is that by getting shot, you may have saved the kid." Lustig stamped out his cigarette. "It's like the Serenity Prayer we say at AA," he said.

"You've been in AA," Langley said.

"Oh, God, yeah, dozens of times," said Lustig, and he said it so good naturedly that they both laughed. "We say, God grant us the ability to change what we can and the wisdom ... no, no, that's not it." Lustig started to mumble to himself. "Anyway, the basic idea is not to sweat the shit you can't change. That's what it says."

He stood and walked over to Langley and clapped him on his bad shoulder. Langley almost fell to the floor in pain. "Oh, Jesus Christ," he said, giving Langley a hand to the couch. "Goddamn it. I'm sorry. Are you OK? Are you all right? Shit, I'm sorry. I totally forgot."

"It's OK. It's OK," said Langley as he lowered himself to the couch, gasping for breath.

"Christ, I'm sorry."

"It's OK," said Langley again, trying to smile.

"OK, Chief." Lustig was trying to hold Langley, trying to make sure he was feeling all right. "Don't, ah, don't sit too long on that couch or you won't be able to get out of it, with that gimpy shoulder."

Langley laughed but he said, "Jesus, don't make me laugh."

"I'm going to get going, Chief."

"I'll talk to you soon."

"When you're ready to go back to work, just give me a call."

"I will, Ed. Thanks. I mean it." Langley was gasping in pain.

Lustig left, muttering to himself and lighting another cigarette.

Thirty

The next day Langley decided to drive by A & J Landfill. He just wanted to get a look at it, the center of so much angst and pain and separation. He couldn't get too close to it, of course. The nearest he could really get without being on the landfill itself was from Antonio Meli's side, but Langley didn't feel like visiting Antonio just now.

He was at the stoplight in the middle of town just after three in the afternoon. The sun was setting to the west, and the light was a sharp, burnished gold.

As he sat at the red light, he looked in this rearview mirror at the driver behind him, a pretty blonde woman wearing sunglasses. She was looking in the direction of the setting sun, and Langley could clearly see every detail of her face. She was running her fingers through her long hair, very slowly, very sensually, and she had a pensive look on her face. Her mouth was set, not quite in a frown. Her skin looked smooth and warm.

Langley had the vague notion that she had just made love or was going to a place where she was about to make love. He wondered why he thought such a thing. He never had those kinds of thoughts. But the woman in the car was attractive—no, alluring—in part because she was so pretty, but also because she seemed so sure of what she was thinking. There was not a doubt in her mind about whatever it was she was thinking. So Langley thought she was going off to make love to someone she loved.

And then he had to let her go. He turned to the left as she went straight and headed down Route 136. As he parked his car on the side of the road, he could see clouds of dust from the earth movers working on top of the ridge.

Very few things in Fenton had engaged its residents like the announcement of the plan to open that landfill in the middle of the town. Fenton had been a sleepy place for decades. Not a single business seemed interested in locating in the town, in part because the Oquossoc didn't have the grandeur or the power of the nearby Piscataqua or Cochecho.

Fenton didn't have empty mill complexes waiting to be gentrified and filled with condos and offices. Town leaders, in their shortsightedness, had torn those down years ago. Other towns that had kept their old mills, either by design or because they simply didn't know what to do with them, had found a revenue stream from office space, condos, restaurants and convention centers. Fenton didn't have that any more.

So the town relied on a network of micro-businesses and worse, the property tax, to cover its costs. Fenton was a mishmash of delis and pizza parlors and one-person graphic design studios. There was one bank branch, three gas stations. There was a florist, who was barely hanging on, and a couple of antique stores. There was one used car lot, but that was really a junkyard zoned as a car lot as a favor to eighty-eight-year-old Dave Jacobs. He was too tired to get rid of the crap on his lawn, and no one wanted to bother with him any more.

Then there were all the unhappy homeowners who twice a year grudgingly paid more in taxes for homes that were seemingly worth less and less.

That's where it stood when Bill Plano first appeared before the Board of Selectmen about ten years ago with his proposal to take a neglected tract of land just off Route 136 and turn it into a landfill.

Plano's application sent him winding through meetings with the zoning board, the zoning board of review, the building committee, the traffic commission, two or three public hearings, and then back to the Board of Selectmen for final approval.

Brian was at Plano's side every step of the way, whispering in his ear, telling Plano who to butter up, who to call to ask for advice so he or she would feel indispensable to this important businessman, and who to invite over to the house for an impromptu cookout so Plano could extol the virtues of living and working in a beautiful town like Fenton.

But it was at the public hearings where alliances and divisions among the town residents were made known. There was no hiding. This was when Langley was a cop in nearby Berwick, Maine, and he felt he could speak his mind freely.

Langley would sit in the audience at the Woodman Middle School while his brother Brian sat at the table in front of the crowd, answering the questions from the public. People in town talked about how the two brothers had taken sides against each other.

The main argument made by Brian and Bill Plano was that the landfill was a business that consumed almost zero resources, and Plano offered the chance of high-paying jobs. The number of jobs he promised at those early meetings was far more than those he actually created. A traffic study commissioned by Brian and Plano proved that traffic would not be increased along Route 136. Langley smiled at this memory. It seems the townspeople had just been told that same thing about the Dirty Books store by the same group of people.

At one meeting Langley asked a question about the number of dump trucks that would be traveling through the center of the town. That was the only thing he said publicly, and Langley got the feeling that Brian had never forgiven him for taking sides.

So now, ten years later, Langley watched the trucks head up the road and into the dry, hot center of the landfill.

Years ago the surface of the landfill wasn't visible from Route 136. It was too far below the trees, but it was now above the lower line of trees, and the company had cut away another twenty acres or more to create another canyon into which they would soon start dumping the next generation of fill. *What else are they dumping up there?* Langley asked himself. Maybe Antonio would find something after all.

LATER THAT DAY Langley pulled into the parking lot of his brother's law office. Brian and his partners had bought an old brick school, the former Wyman School for Girls, a squat Federal style building. It was an elegant structure spoiled by the sign Brian had bought for the firm. It was a big, boxy, rectangular thing, lit from inside with fluorescent bulbs. Black and red lettering in italics that made the names look like they should have been on the side of a racecar.

Langley was in a foul mood when he was let into Brian's office. He told Brian he intended to find out what happened on Antonio Meli's property.

"I don't give a shit what you do, Langley," said Brian. "You do what you want, only I'd think you'd want to do something useful with your life. This seems like a hobby, a pastime. Trivia. Nobody cares anymore."

Brian was standing behind his desk, which was an old oak door from a farmhouse in Fenton, torn down when they were kids. Brian had a picture of him and Danny on the shelf behind him. Brian stood at his desk when he worked. He said it relaxed him, but Langley thought Brian did it because it made him look imperious.

"It's the one thing I've left hanging."

"That is hardly the one thing you've left hanging, brother."

"You just don't ever miss an opportunity to be an asshole," said Langley.

"As I said, if this makes you happy. I appreciate you coming to tell me. But really, what does this have to do with me?"

Langley sighed a deep, heavy sigh.

"All right. Never mind. Dad wants us all to come over for dinner," Brian said.

"I said I would. I'm free any night."

"OK, maybe Thursday. I don't think the kids have anything that night." Brian paused. "What are you going to do for Thanksgiving?"

"I thought I'd go over to Dad's. What are you doing?"

"We're going to go to the Bluefin, I guess," which was a restaurant Brian's family went to on Thanksgiving. His wife was a great cook, but she hated to cook on the big holidays. "You can come if you want, if you don't want to be the third wheel with Dad and his girlfriend."

Langley marveled at how Brian could turn even a seemingly genuine invitation into a way to take a little jab. "Or I might just take a bottle of cyanide," he said.

"Choose your poison," Brian said cheerfully. "Look, good luck duck hunting. I hope you find your prey."

Thirty-One

Langley was on I-95 heading north to Berlo, Maine. Berlo was a tiny town on the Canadian border. There was nothing up there except unemployment and a man named Jefferson Prince. This was a name given to Langley by a friend of a friend of a friend of Ed Lustig's, and Langley was told this guy knew something about animal trafficking.

Langley was so far north the towns no longer had names, they were identified by numbers. He had been on the road for hours, and it was just past ten o'clock. He was traveling behind an old Ford station wagon that had a bumper sticker that said Magic Happens and another that said The Goddess Is Alive and Magic Is Afoot and still another, You're A Hemorrhoid.

Clouds had rolled in from the east. When he left Fenton rain was falling out of the dark, heavy clouds off in the distance, and now they were right on top of him. Langley was comforted by the sound of the first raindrops that slapped against his windshield.

As a kid he remembered watching the patterns falling raindrops made in the puddles in the backyard. When it rained on a warm day, he never went inside, and his mother never called for him to come in. He would let the rain soak through his clothes so the fabric clung to his skin, and he liked the feeling of the drops against his face. He could sit on the porch of his parents' house and watch the rain for hours as though it was the most entertaining movie in the world.

Frank Sinatra came on the radio. It was a version of “Sunny,” an unusual song. “Sunny one so true, I love you.” When Sinatra sang the line, "Thank you for the sunshine bouquet," the image of Delia Reed's face floated up in front of him, and Langley knew that he was in love with her.

Northern Maine is a lonely place. Miles and miles of road with nothing to look except pine trees and lakes and deer. If Langley hadn't been so familiar with this old New England landscape, he might have been frightened by the loneliness and wildness of it.

The voice on his GPS brought him to a little side street in Berlo. He parked in front of a pizza shop that was also listed as the address for Prince.

Langley got out of his car and went up to what looked like a door to a stairway leading to the apartment above the pizza parlor. There was no buzzer, so Langley knocked. There was no answer. He stepped back to look up at the building. As he looked down at his feet to make sure that he didn't fall off the curb, Langley noticed the gutter was filled with crushed and decomposing bird feathers. He stared for a second, concerned about what that could mean, and then walked back up to the door and knocked again.

A window on the second floor opened, and a man with a beard stuck his head out.

"Calhoun?"

"Yes, sir," said Langley.

"The door's unlocked. Come right in." The window shut.

Langley went in. The stairwell was filled with the aroma of baking pizzas. He walked up the narrow, dark stairs and stepped around a wheelchair lift as he pushed open the one door that was available to him. He got the creeps as soon as he walked into the room. It wasn't messy, or cluttered, but it was an uncomfortable place.

Jefferson Prince was sitting in a wheelchair. Langley couldn't make out his age because his skin and his limbs had withered. Prince looked at Langley through eyeglasses that should have had their prescription updated years and years ago. The glasses were filthy, and so was Jefferson Prince.

His teeth were black and cracked. His fingernails were black and cracked. His long, greasy hair was pulled back in a ponytail. He had a bowl full of some kind of food in his lap. The big wall behind Prince had graffiti scrawled on it. There were three words printed in an Old English typeface: *Strix occidentalis caurina.* Langley automatically assumed it was a kind of white supremacy slogan written in Latin. Just below those words was a huge, crudely drawn Christian cross.

"Jefferson Prince?"

"That's me. You're Langley, the cop who got shot working for Ed Lustig."

"I'm not a cop anymore."

"Private detective then."

"Private investigator," Langley said, smiling.

"Oh, please," said the withered man. He looked at Langley. He was hunched over. He looked crab-like, suspicious, and ready to fall from his wheelchair and scuttle away sideways. The entire apartment smelled like a cage soaked in urine and feces.

"If there's one thing I can't stand, it's a rotten grape," Prince said, fingering a piece of sodden food in his hand.

"What?"

"Have you ever bitten into anything so disgusting as a rotten grape?" The man was pawing through the food in his bowl. "Rotten grapes, overripe bananas, boiled raisins," the man muttered. "Those things I can't stand."

"I understand you know a little something about animal trafficking," Langley said loudly. "I'm wondering if you can help me."

"No, no," said the man.

"No?"

"I'll ask the questions." Prince put the bowl on a small table. "And you don't have to shout. I'm dying, but I'm not deaf."

The man took out a pack of unfiltered Camels. *Christ,* thought Langley, *I thought everybody was supposed to have quit smoking.* Prince lit it up and turned on one of those ashtrays that was supposed to suck the smoke and the odor out of the air, but by the stench in the room it was obvious it didn't work.

"What makes you think you're involved with the illegal trafficking of animals?"

"First of all, I'm not involved," said Langley. "I'm interested in the possibility of rare animal trafficking, and Ed Lustig says you may know something about it."

"It was a crowned solitary eagle, eh?" said Prince.

"Yes."

"From South America."

"Correct."

"Not a very good looking animal," said Prince.

Langley was standing about ten feet away from this man, who had not yet asked him to sit. He was tired, so he moved over to the chair that was closest to him, a simple wooden kitchen chair, and sat. *God help me,* he thought. He took out his small notebook and a pencil and wrote down the Latin phrase that was written on the wall. He'd look that up later.

"What is so important about this crowned eagle?" Jefferson Prince asked.

"Nothing very much, I suppose, only that it was killed in my town under my watch, and I'm interested in finding out who did it."

"Is that all?"

"No."

"What else?"

"I suppose I want to know why. Why it was there. Why someone would do such a thing."

Prince sat rolling his burning cigarette between his fingers. "The police, they ... the question of why is of secondary interest to the police, isn't that right?"

"I suppose so," said Langley. "We want to know who did something first, and then the why, if it matters."

Prince chuckled, but it was a derisive chuckle. Langley knew what Prince meant. Langley was a cog in the police state, a thug not interested in humanity or the causes of crime. He was just an armed fascist.

Prince looked up at Langley. "But in this case you're interested in why it happened."

"It seems so senseless."

The old man cackled. "It wasn't senseless to the perpetrator." Prince blew out a huge plume of blue smoke. "If you were of a criminal bent, and I don't know if you are or aren't, one of the best crimes you can get involved in would be the trafficking of exotic animals. Do you know why?"

"Because it's hard to track."

"Exactly right. And they're only animals. Do people know you're still working on this?"

"I don't know."

"Because if they do know, you're going to have them worried. Chances are this isn't the only bit of illegality they're involved in. So I would watch out, if I were you, if you continue."

"Mafia?"

"Not just the one mafia anymore, Mr. Calhoun, those were the good old days. If the police have been successful in wiping out the Italian mafia, it has more to do with the mob's inability to adapt than for any successful tactics employed by you people. Because now you have the Russian mafia, the Chinese, the Japanese, the Latino gangs, they're all thriving. Not to mention the millions of solitary criminals who are just trying to go about their business. So you failed miserably."

"I'm not sure these people are in Fenton."

"Oh, there's the Italian mafia, too, still hanging on, so you never know. The Chinese, the Russians, certainly couldn't hide in your little town, but a member of the Italian mob I imagine could still fit in."

"What can you tell me about how birds are transported?" Langley was doodling in his notebook.

"It isn't really so complicated. The traffickers simply mix up the exotic and illegal with the legal and documented cargo. The airlines don't care. You think the feds are going to interrupt international flights over birds and snakes? Do you know what kind of havoc that would cause?" Prince shook his head. He seemed rueful, sad. Whatever activism he may have had about the subject had long ago dissipated. "So if you have a shipment of parrots and turtles and snakes, all perfectly legal, all you have to do is throw in a few exotic species, and no one will care to look. There's always bribery, too, to help things run smoothly."

Langley sighed. He didn't have to ask a question. He knew Prince would keep talking. He was an old teacher, after all, showing off his knowledge.

"The law was a good law, at first it was a good law," said Prince.

Langley didn't look up from his notebook. There was something tragic about this old man. "What law?"

"The Endangered Species Act," said Prince. "Covers everything. You can't fuck with birds, mammals, plants, amphibians, and now it covers mollusks, crustaceans. That's right. Invertebrates." Prince seemed slightly offended by the notion. "But the law covers everything without funding anything." He spat a bit of tobacco off his tongue. "No one has any money. Not the country where the animals are taken from, not the place where they are taken to. Back in the day, the feds hardly had any biologists on staff, hardly any at all." He mumbled something.

"Excuse me," said Langley.

"Not that they wanted my help," Prince said.

"How many, um, how many animals are …"

"Oh, please. Who can know? One million animals a year worth how much? A hundred million? A billion a year? How does anybody know these things? Whatever you hear on that score will be wrong. The point is, it's pervasive."

Prince stamped out his cigarette in the ashtray and as quickly lit another.

"You take the birds right out of the nest, and so two things happen. You're able to transport them when they're small and quiet, but you also keep thinning the ranks. Each succeeding generation gets smaller and smaller because there are no mature members of the species, none old enough to breed. How do you track the number of chicks taken from a nest in a tree in the Amazon Basin in Ecuador?"

"You can't," said Langley. The two sat quietly for a moment.

"The goddamn fucking federal government," Prince said, his head bobbing back and forth like a chicken. When he said that Langley knew instantly what had happened to Jefferson Prince's career. He had probably always been an eccentric, but then something snapped, and his views became more and more untenable. Maybe he was never tenured. A smart man, but not smart enough or not disciplined enough, his published works too infrequent and too inconsequential to matter.

So he compensated by being the loudest, the most radical, the most inflammatory, using rhetorical flourishes to hide the thinness of his intellect. But then, over time, flush with continued slights from the academic and publishing worlds, Prince's road show act morphed into something undeniably real, and so he was jettisoned from his college community. Maybe he suffered a succession of lesser and lesser posts until he was reduced to living off Social Security checks, pecking out his final days in a community where the locals have rumored him to be some famous professor from Harvard or Yale, a rumor he never disputes.

But there was no *Tuesdays with Morrie* adulation from former students, no tributes. There was just a slow slide from irrelevance to criminality, which brought Jefferson Prince into contact with Ed Lustig and now with Langley.

"I don't mind them trying to protect that natural world," said Prince, "but not through any means necessary." *Ah,* thought Langley, *a hint of the old campus radicalism.* But what Jefferson Prince didn't know was that this kind of talk was on TV and on the radio and the Internet hourly, and it had lost its punch.

"Them who?" asked Langley.

"You can't tell people what to do with their private lands. That's sacred, so it was natural," said Prince, "to reject, to react against, that which you think is unjust."

"React against who?" But Langley knew, so he answered his own question. "You're not in favor of the ESA allowing the feds to dictate protecting these species on private property."

"That's exactly right," said Prince. "Fascists." He spat out the word and squinted in Langley's direction to see what the reaction would be. But that word didn't mean anything anymore, either.

"The government doesn't want to protect the animals, but it wants you to," said Prince. "That's when I gave up on the whole thing."

"Is there trafficking of illegal animals through New Hampshire and Maine?" asked Langley.

"Of course there is. These places see their fair share of everything, just like everyplace else. They bring it up through customs here at the border, which is not exactly like breaking into Fort Knox, and they can get them over to Europe from Canada," said Prince. "But also you have to remember. Not every bird or animal is sent to decadent Europe. Many of them end up right here in the good old corrupt US of A."

He took a long drag off his cigarette. Langley closed his notebook. Prince suddenly sat up. He didn't think he was going to lose his audience so soon.

"You found a dead bird. Here's the thing. Ninety percent of all animals that are illegally transported die. Do you know why? They tape their beaks shut, they gouge their eyes out so they won't sing to the sun, they stuff them into socks and small boxes."

"And?"

"And? Well, a dead bird is just as dangerous to a criminal as a live bird. You've got to find a place to put it. But I suspect that whoever is disposing of their dead cargo isn't being terribly discreet about it because they think no one is looking." Prince looked Langley over.

"You say that no one cares, but I'll worry people if they find out I'm looking into it," said Langley. "Which is it?"

"No one on the law enforcement side cares," said Prince. He seemed to boil with rage at being misunderstood. "The traffickers very much care. If you can't understand that much ..."

"I understand," said Langley. "I misunderstood you before."

"They're used to moving about with impunity," said Prince. "You're going to upset their rhythm and, more importantly, their money, and they won't like that."

Langley stood. "Do you know anybody in this business?" asked Langley.

"I can't answer that," said Prince, but Langley knew he didn't know anything practical.

"I hope that our conversation stays private and my identity stays private," said Langley.

Prince had an inscrutable expression on his face. "There's much more you should know about this, Mr. Calhoun." Prince picked up his bowl from the table next to him. "Would you like a cup of coffee? I'm afraid I haven't been a very good host. We could share a pizza."

"No, I've heard enough," said Langley. He put his notebook in his pocket. He was headed toward the door.

"I'm glad you care," said Prince.

Langley thought he sounded sincere, so he said, "I do care."

Then, in the most condescending voice imaginable, Jefferson Prince said, "Maybe if you find who killed the bird, you'll atone for all your sins."

WHEN HE GOT DOWN TO HIS CAR, Langley leaned against the door and dialed Ed Lustig's number and got his voicemail. "Hey, Lustig, it's Langley Calhoun. I'm not going to say thank you for having me drive all the way up to Berlo to see some guy out of *Deliverance*."

Langley stopped talking because just at that moment a multi-colored bird feather whirly-gigged right down past his face and landed in the gutter. It startled him, and Langley looked up to see where it came from. Jefferson Prince was leaning out his window with a smirk on his face. When he knew that Langley had seen him, he cackled and disappeared back into the window.

"I just want you to know, Ed, that I could have gone my whole life without meeting that guy," Langley said. Then he closed the phone and got the hell out of Berlo, Maine.

Thirty-Two

Langley had called Antonio to ask him if he had any idea about how to keep the heat on A & J Gravel. Antonio let him know a few days later that he had an idea and asked him to come over so he could tell him about it. He also asked Langley to pick him up a new pair of binoculars on his way over.

When Langley came into Antonio's house, Antonio was enjoying his daily black and tan. "People get away with too much shit simply because we don't take the time to look," Antonio said. He also said he was going to monitor the activity at A & J Fill & Gravel. He would record anything and everything. He was going to write down and research the names of the companies coming in and out of the landfill. He was determined to drill as deeply into the origins of that company as he possibly could.

"The police can't do it," he concluded.

"And one of the reasons they can't is that no one wants to fund the force," said Langley. Antonio was one of the people in town who had voted against increased funding for the police.

"What I mean to say is they won't do it," said Antonio. "They tell me there has to be evidence of a crime."

"You follow that reasoning, don't you?"

Antonio said he had written down the names of all the employees listed on the A & J website. He was going to look up each one and find out where they came from and if they had anything that could remotely be connected to the eagle. He was going to record the name of all the companies dropping off their debris at the landfill and track them down, as well.

"What if I find out that the head of one of these companies going in and out of the landfill used to work in a zoo in Acapulco?" He smiled when he said that.

Langley raised an eyebrow. He almost laughed. Antonio was joking, but he had a point.

"We'll just try to see what's going on behind the corporate posture," said Antonio.

Langley nodded. He knew of all the ways that Plano and the company supported the town. They were highly regarded. A & J had a good reputation. The company's website reflected that. There were no photos of concrete mountains or of the crater that had cut a scar through the hillsides of Fenton. Rather, there were photographs of rolling hills and the usual corporate-speak about how A& J was a local company and one that was dedicated to the most stringent environmental policies and practices. The company owned other landfills in other towns, and everyone, everywhere, seemed to love them.

The parent company had been honored by various groups, but Langley knew these were simply the awards that were given out by self-regulating industries in order to look somewhat respectable to outsiders. Public relations pap.

There wasn't even a way to contact the business through the website. There was just an 800 number that was answered with a pre-taped business message. They didn't want anyone calling them.

Langley also knew this: None of the businesses bringing in the demolished remains of old buildings to the landfill cared about awards and plaques. They just needed a place to bring their shit. Handing over the binoculars and goggles, Langley reminded Meli that what he was doing was no joke.

"Goddamn it, Chief, I know these people can hurt me, but I'm an old man."

"How long are you willing to keep this up?" said Langley.

"I'm willing," said Antonio. Langley was full of admiration for the old man. He had always respected him, ever since he heard him tell the story about his time in Korea.

"You cannot get caught," said Langley. "If there's something going on up there, and they find out you're watching them ..."

"I'm not gonna try to hide," said Antonio.

"Well, where are you going to conduct this high-tech stake out?"

"About a hundred feet back from the property line is a huge old bull pine," said Antonio. "I'll sit up high in one of the branches. It's the perfect place."

"You can't climb up that old pine," said Langley.

"You help me up, you help me down. We'll be fine."

Antonio was asking Langley to climb up into a tree. He broke out in a cold sweat.

Thirty-Three

Langley was trying to keep at bay every demon that had ever plagued him since his brother's death. He was trying to stay calm. He had not climbed a tree in almost thirty years, and he had vowed he would never climb a tree again after what had happened to Danny. So far, he hadn't.

He was carrying the binoculars for Antonio, supposedly to assist the old man, but Meli was four or five paces ahead of Langley as they walked up the hill. They reached the huge bull pine. The trunk was huge.

"Let me show you how strong this tree is," said Antonio. "Look at this." He pointed to a notch that ringed the entire circumference at the base of the tree. The notch was about six inches wide. "They say that if you cut off the bark entirely around the whole tree, you'll cut off its food supply, right? And it'll die, right? So I cut a belt out of the bark, all the way around. You see? I did that with a hatchet. That was in 1971, and the tree isn't dead yet," said Antonio. He shook his head. The thing of it was that Meli was full of admiration for the tree, and just as Langley was thinking this, Antonio said, "I'm sorry I tried to kill it, and if I cut short its life, I am truly sorry." Antonio patted the bark of the old pine and looked up. "Let's go," he said.

They propped up a small step ladder that got Antonio onto the first huge limb, and Langley watched as the old man scrambled to step up on top of it. Antonio grabbed another branch above his head and elegantly lifted himself to the next tier.

Langley went up the ladder and handed Antonio the binoculars. *Goddamn that old man,* Langley thought to himself. He had flop sweat dripping down into his eyes, and he was breathing quickly and shallowly as he steadied himself at the top of the little ladder. He was trying to stop the screaming from overwhelming him.

Antonio had a shit-eating grin on his face because he thought the chief just couldn't cut it. "What were you, in the navy?" he said and laughed at his own joke.

Langley lifted up Antonio's old canteen and a Ziploc bag full of raw almonds and dried cranberries, which were Antonio's favorite snacks.

"All right, Chief, you go take a nap," said Antonio with more than a little mischief in his voice. "You look as though you need it."

"I'm OK," said Langley.

"Oh, no you're not," said Antonio, and Langley remembered that he was talking to a guy who had been in active combat in Korea and knew a few things about how to look out for himself.

Christ, thought Langley, *he should have been with me when I got shot.* "Listen," he said, "don't think for one second about climbing down by yourself, and if you think you're going to fall asleep, call me." They had their cell phones.

"I'll be OK, Chief," said Antonio. He scrambled up another twenty feet. Langley got off the ladder and looked up. *Goddamn that old man,* he thought again.

"I can see pretty well from right here," Antonio called down.

Langley walked down to Antonio's house. He was exhausted, and he was trying to decide whether to tell Antonio why he had been so nervous up in the tree, but he knew that telling the story would only be to save face. He also knew that Antonio may have understood. There were not many old-timers in town who didn't know the story about Danny.

Langley was shocked at how powerful and raw his feelings were, how fresh. When he went back to Antonio's house he flopped down on the couch and listened to the screams inside his head. He didn't try to shut them out.

Thirty-Four

Langley woke with a start on Antonio's couch. It was a little after 7:00 p.m. *Jesus,* he thought, *Antonio's been out there all day.*

He hurried to the tree and immediately realized he shouldn't have worried. He saw Antonio sitting on the lowest limb, just sitting there dangling his legs like a little kid. He was grinning.

"Jesus Christ, Antonio. I'm sorry. You must be sore as hell."

"Nope."

Langley put the step ladder up against the tree. "Did you see anything?"

"After the workers go home, the kids come out," said Antonio. "They come up to drink and smoke. But I made a note of all the businesses that came in. I've got some info to start with."

Langley guided Antonio down. "Are you all right?"

"Yeah, a little stiff, but I'm fine."

"I fell asleep," said Langley.

"Not even a problem."

"You're not going to be able to keep this up," said Langley.

"Oh, yes I am." They walked back to the house.

THE NEXT DAY, ANTONIO HAD a bag slung over his shoulder filled with blocks of wood. Langley was right behind him, shaking his head. Antonio wanted to do his surveillance in comfort. They reached the old bull pine, and Antonio put his stuff down on the ground.

"I'm going to build some steps and also make a little chair right where those two branches come together, right up there," Antonio said, pointing. "Get myself a little comfort."

Langley just shook his head and smiled. A few hours later, Antonio had crafted a ladder made out of blocks that ascended the trunk of the pine. There was also a nice little lounge chair propped up against the trunk of the tree about a hundred feet above them. The chair looked relatively comfortable.

"Antonio, your talents never cease to amaze me," said Langley.

"I'll come back up here tomorrow," Antonio said. "Now I'll take a nap."

Thirty-Five

"What a crew," said Ed Lustig to Langley. "I'm on eight different medications. I need a pill planner, for Christ sake. I've got hypertension, fat in the blood, sugar. You've got one good arm, and your surveillance expert is an eighty-five-year-old man who thinks he's an Indian living in a tree."

Lustig was sitting in desk chair smoking a cigarette and drinking Bushmills.

"Antonio is eighty-two," said Langley with a smile.

"Well, then, sign him up for the Olympics." Ed laughed a big burst of a laugh. "Why don't you forget it and just come back here. I've got some work I need to get done."

"What work?"

"Some filing."

"Very funny."

"All I'm saying is you're not equipped. Give it up."

"I'm not doing anything hardly," said Langley. "Antonio's off on his own."

"Sitting in a goddamn tree."

"True, true."

"So tell me what he's doing?"

"He takes down all the names of the companies that deliver at the landfill."

"And how is he doing that again?"

Langley sighed. He knew Ed was busting his balls. He had already told him the story, but Lustig got some kind of laugh out of hearing it again. "Antonio sits up in his little perch, and he reads off the names on the sides of the trucks that come in to deliver at the landfill."

"This is like a very sophisticated military strategy."

"Come on, Ed."

Lustig sighed. "Go on."

"Then he looks them up and tries to find everything about them, anything at all."

"And the point is?"

"Antonio's trying to find a connection to anything. He's looking for wrongdoing anywhere. If there's any connection to anyone with any kind of bird trafficking, any kind of animal trafficking. Jefferson Prince said that traffickers have to worry about dead animals as much as live ones, so we just figured the solitary crowned eagle was dumped there, already dead, and dragged off the property by some animal, a fox, whatever. I mean, I admit it's cockamamie, but I'll support him. I told you I want to find out what happened to the bird, too."

Lustig smoked for a little while. He took a sip of his drink and when he realized his glass was empty, he reached for the bottle on his desk and poured out a couple of fingers more.

"OK," he said. He looked into his glass. "It isn't the worst idea in the world."

"Because no one else is paying attention, and you never know what you might see."

"That's true," said Lustig, who then had a wicked gleam in his eye, "as long as he doesn't decide to follow them into Home Depot."

Even Langley had to laugh, but as he did, he rubbed his shoulder.

"But so far nothing," said Lustig.

"Nothing to connect one dot to anything else, and now Antonio keeps seeing the same companies, more or less."

"So you're winding down?"

"It looks that way."

"Anyway, it's not who's dumping at the landfill. It's what they're dumping, right?"

"You're probably right," said Langley.

"You'd have to find a way to sample the shit that people are bringing in. You'd have to find another dead animal. But anything you took would be inadmissible, if you or your old man didn't get shot first."

"I know," said Langley.

"Well, you never know what you'll find if you just watch," Lustig said.

After another week Langley told Antonio to quit. Nothing was happening.

Thirty-Six

Friday, October 29, 6:00 p.m. "What are you going to be for Halloween?"

This was a torturous conversation. Langley was on the phone with his oldest child, and their sentences were interspersed with long, painful silences. Neither of them could think of anything to say, but what Langley heard next pained him.

"I don't dress up for Halloween, anymore, Dad," his daughter Patty said, voice dripping with contempt.

Christ, thought Langley, but then he said to himself, *keep trying. And be honest.* "Well, sometimes I forget just how much time has gone by"

"Mom!" the voice on the other end of the phone rang out. Langley heard "What?" in the background, and then the voices on the other end were muffled. Obviously, the phone was changing hands.

"It seems as though the conversation is over," said Julia, his ex-wife.

"It certainly seems that way."

"How are you feeling?" she asked. Langley was beginning to hate that question.

"Fine. You know."

"Fine? Really? You lose half your shoulder and it feels fine?"

"I just meant that ..."

"I've got to go clean up. We're going to a basketball game tonight."

"Listen!" Langley shouted into the phone. He didn't mean to shout, but he wanted to say something, he wanted to be heard. "The reason I said that I felt fine was because I don't want to ... I wanted to say I'm fine because it always seems as though I'm in ..."

"Trouble?" finished his ex-wife. "Or in some kind of silent, existential crisis that no one knows about?" Julia drew in a deep breath. "The reason," she said, mimicking his tone of just a moment ago, "that I ask is because I care. You were shot. The kids, even through all their anger, were scared. They cried. They didn't know what to do. You are still their father."

Langley listened.

"Your vagueness, Langley, that's a burden. Your silences are a burden. Telling me that you're in pain or your life sucks and you want to feel better, that would be fine. I'd welcome that."

There was another silence.

"Fine." She sighed again. "Langley. I love you. The girls love you." The words were kind, but the tone was angry. "You don't have a family anymore, but you should."

His heart was breaking, and yet still he said nothing.

Julia hung up.

Thirty-Seven

Saturday, October 30, 8:30 a.m. The day of the Halloween parade was bright, the sky was a clear, pale blue, and the ground was covered with crisp, dry leaves.

Langley woke and stretched, showered and shaved, and drove himself over to Ruggerio's Market for a cup of coffee and the newspaper. The front page of *The Fenton Herald* was filled with the momentous news of that day's parade. The huge headline simply said SPOOKY!

While Langley was reading the paper in the small cafe at the market, the new chief of police, Ted Darrow, walked over to say hello.

"Chief," he said.

"Chief," Langley nodded.

"Do you mind if I sit?"

"Of course not," said Langley, folding up his paper.

Chief Darrow sat down, holding his cup of coffee. He looked at Langley and said, "Some of the guys told me you hang out here in the morning."

"My little routine," said Langley.

"I've been meaning to call you."

"I've been wondering why you haven't, but I understand the process. You want to do things your own way."

"Yes, but I could have used a tutorial on a few things."

Langley smiled. "On the Fenton way, you mean."

"Yes," said the chief. "You have your own way here."

"We certainly do." Langley paused. "How are you getting along with Maria Tull?"

They both laughed. "The politics of a small town," said the new chief.

"At least I was born here," said Langley. "You'll never be anything but a visitor."

"I'll never be anything but the hired help," said the new chief, sipping his coffee and looking around. "I get the feeling they like hiring someone from the outside because they consider what I do their dirty work. They're too proud to pick up after themselves. It's either that or they hire someone they have no respect for."

This was obviously something the new chief had been told, but he had not meant to say it out loud. There was an awkward silence. "That didn't come out right," he said to Langley.

"Oh, yes it did," said Langley, and they laughed a little.

"The parade is a pretty big deal, I guess," said the new chief.

"The whole town will be there," said Langley. "Scary puppets." Langley held up the local paper and mocked the headline. "Spooky," he said.

The new chief smiled. "Listen, I heard about what happened to you," said Darrow. "I heard versions of what happened to you when they let you go. I'm sorry. I think that was rough."

"It depends on what you heard."

"I heard that you had pissed off some people."

"Pissed off my brother and his clients."

"Right," said the chief, looking at Langley. "I'm inclined," he said slowly, "to just get my sea legs here and not get too ahead of myself before I step into anything that may disrupt the flow."

Langley knew what he meant. "I've got a little news for you. I've been looking for evidence that A&J Fill & Gravel is doing something wrong, anything wrong, for the past two weeks and I come up with zero, so I think you can in all good conscience let it go. It was a hunch borne out of bad blood between a lot of people, and it won't lead anywhere," said Langley. "It's done. You're not neglecting anything if you let it go."

"I appreciate that," said the new chief.

"I was operating under only the slightest hunch, a rumor, and not even that, if you want to know the truth," Langley said. "My feeling is that something a little odd happened when Antonio Meli found that bird, and maybe it spurred my imagination. I don't know."

"What's next?"

"If there's anything going on up there, let the feds take care of it. They have the muscle. It's their problem. If the shit hits the fan, they have the luxury of not living here. They can disappear." Langley paused. "Time for a new adventure."

"OK," said the new chief, rising. He reached out to shake Langley's hand. "Again, I'm sorry I didn't call you. I don't mean that I'm sorry if that appeared rude, I mean that, given what I've learned the hard way, I'm really sorry I didn't call you." Langley accepted the outstretched hand.

"Forget about it."

"Let's get together sometime, have a drink. You can take me on a tour."

"I'll probably see you at the parade tonight," said Langley.

"You bet."

They parted, and Langley decided he liked the new chief.

LANGLEY TOOK A DEEP BREATH and picked up his phone. There was a foolish knot that had tied itself in his stomach. He was going to call Delia Reed. *Christ,* he thought, *I can step into a domestic dispute and not think twice about it, but this unnerves me.*

He looked at his watch. It wasn't too early to call. He took a deep breath and pushed a button.

"Well, hello there Mr. Calhoun."

He didn't like the way she said that. Was she joking? "Hey Delia. How are you?"

"I'm good. How are you?"

"I'm feeling pretty good, you know. It still feels funny, but ..."

"No, no, how are you really?"

"You know, I think I'm all right."

"That's good. I'm glad to hear it. That's what I wanted to hear." She paused. Langley had not called her since the day he saw her in the hospital, and she had cried. He didn't know if he had damaged things completely.

"Listen, um, I was going to head over to my dad's house." For some reason as he was saying this, he had squeezed his eyes tight, as though he was willing Delia Reed to answer yes to his question. "We were going to have a little cookout and couple of cocktails before we headed over to the parade, and I was wondering if you wanted to come over."

She sighed. Langley did not like that sound. She sighed again. "I should be mad," she said. "It's the day of the parade."

"I know, I know," said Langley softly with his eyes still squeezed shut.

But then she said, "Sure, I'd love to." Her voice was suddenly filled with warmth.

"You're not, you don't ..."

"What time?"

Langley hadn't even thought of that. What time? "Eleven or so?"

"I'll meet you at your dad's house at eleven, OK?"

"Great, yes, good." Langley was beaming. "All right then. I'll see you then."

"Langley!"

"Oh, the address."

"If you don't mind, kind sir." She had a lovely voice. After she had written down the address, she said, "I'm glad you called."

Thirty-Eight

"So I'm pulling out of the gas station, and I had to wait because the traffic was so heavy," said Delia Reed, "and I had it on WHEB, and they were playing 'Lola.'"

"That is my favorite song," said Timothy Calhoun.

"I love that song, too," said Delia. "So there's a guy stuck at the red light, he's about thirty feet from me, I can see him clear as a bell, and he's obviously listening to the same station, because he's over there, singing like he's Ray Davies. The guy's about fifty, and he's reliving his youth. He's got the top down, he's got his sweater tied in a knot around his neck, and you can tell he doesn't really know the words." Everybody laughed at the image. "He's absolutely belting out the song. The things people do in their cars."

"Tell me about it," said Tim Calhoun while simultaneously offering a lascivious wink in Vance's direction.

"Oh, please, Dad," said Brian, but everyone was laughing.

Delia Reed was right at home in Timothy Calhoun's living room. They had all wanted to sit on the porch, but the day turned cool so they sat inside. Brian and Eileen were there, and little Emily and Danny, and Vance, who had elected to make hors d'oeuvres.

"How did you decide to become a park ranger?" Eileen asked Delia.

"You know, my parents were hippies. I mean, real hippies, but there was only one flaw in their thinking when they decided to live that kind of life. They had no money."

Everybody laughed again.

"No trust fund," said Brian.

"That's right," said Delia. "My parents had no money. Gaia will provide."

"Gaia?" said Langley.

"Mother Earth," said Delia. "That was their word. Gaia, the Earth Goddess."

"Earth is a woman," said Brian somewhat dismissively.

Delia heard the tone, but she ignored it. "I subscribe to the notion, the idea of it."

"I think it's a beautiful word," said Vance.

"So life was hard, and we drifted around. My parents tried to sell their crafts, and they tried to grow what they ate, but it was never very successful. But—and this was the thing—they both truly loved being outdoors. They were very knowledgeable about nature."

"Are both your parents still living?" asked Brian, eating a Triscuit with avocado and brie.

"No, they both passed away within a year of each other. My father had leukemia, and my mother had breast cancer," Delia Reed said.

"I'm sorry to hear that," said Eileen.

"They taught me to love nature, to protect nature, but I also knew that I would also like to have a steady job," said Delia, and everybody chuckled. "So, U.S. Park Ranger."

"Did they live long enough to see you go to work for the guv-ment," said Brian in an inappropriately jokey way.

"They saw me go to UNH and graduate, and then I went to work in Colorado, where I spent time as a kid. When they both got sick, I came back here to care for them."

"It's nice to have you here," said Eileen, pressing her hand into Delia's.

"I think it would be wonderful to work outdoors. It must have a kind of freedom," said Vance. "Half the time I sit at my desk looking out the window, thinking I'd like to go into landscaping. You know, sit on one of those rider mowers with the handles." More laughter from the group.

"What do you do, Vance? Is it Vance? That's an unusual name," said Delia.

"Oh, my God," she said. "Your parents were hippies. My parents were television freaks, and they loved *I Love Lucy*, but they especially loved Vivian Vance, for whatever reason. You know, the actress who played Ethel Mertz?"

"That's who you're named after?" blurted Timothy.

Vance mock-glared at the old man. "Do you think that makes me less sexy?" When the elder Calhoun hesitated for a second, she erupted into giggles. "You do, don't you? Ha! My new boyfriend is now stuck with pictures of Ethel Mertz in his head."

"Don't. Stop it," Timothy Calhoun said, comically putting his hands over his eyes and ears.

"You'll have to double up on that dose of Levitra," Vance joked.

"Don't say that in front of my kids," said the old man. "They're just children."

"Your dad takes pharmaceuticals," said Vance, cupping her mouth with her hands. "Thank God," she added, and they all laughed again.

"I think that's something Brian ought to take every now and again," said Eileen. She meant it as a joke, but she just sort of blurted it out, bringing the conversation to a screeching halt.

"Well, that's a ..." Brian started to say but simply stopped in mid-sentence.

Vance rescued the situation by saying, "And to answer your question, I'm head of HR over at Mutual Insurance."

"How do you like that?" asked Langley in what still seemed like a deathly quiet room.

"Let me just say—oh, thank you, Sweetie." Old man Calhoun had just handed Vance another drink, and his face was beet red. "You have to sit there and listen to people who have the most tangled relationships with each other and with the company. As an HR person you can't really say anything anymore. You're not allowed. You make neutral statements to people like: 'I can see how you could think that from your perspective,' and everything is designed to make the person think that they've been heard. But we're so lawyered up," Vance sighed. "I don't really want to talk about work."

"Neither do any of us," said Brian, standing. "Besides, I have to get dressed."

This year Brian had been selected to play Sam Hain, the mythical leader of The Parade of the Horribles. His job was to stand on an open flatbed truck, declaring the end of summer, and to invoke the spirits to thank them for a bountiful harvest and ask for a better one the following year. Sam Hain wore a traditional costume, a crown of small gourds and apples and a garment of corn stalks and pumpkin leaves. It was actually felt cloth that had been cut to resemble leaves.

Brian got up to change, and Langley poured himself and Delia another glass of wine.

"This is some kind of parade you do every year," said Vance.

"Oh, the whole town shows up," said Eileen. "Everybody will be there."

After a few minutes Brian walked into the living room wearing his costume.

"You should wear that to court," said Timothy. "You might get somewhere."

"I never really realized just how ridiculous this thing is," said Brian.

"You campaigned for the job," said Langley.

"Well, let's just get this farce over with," said Brian. "Let's go."

They all started to gather their things when Delia said, "Hey, Langley." He was picking up some paper plates when he looked up. "Can you give me a quick tour of the house before we head over? I'd like to see it."

"Oh, yeah, yeah, um, I'd love to. Do you guys mind waiting a bit? "

"We'll just go right on ahead," said Eileen while handing her kids their coats. "You two can meet up with us later." She smiled a warm, beautiful smile at Delia.

Everybody left, and the house was silent. Langley just stood and stared at Delia. It was very, very quiet.

Thirty-Nine

"So," Delia said after everyone had gone, "this is where you grew up."

Langley looked up at the ceiling, anticipating taking Delia through the rooms upstairs where he and Brian and Danny had once slept. Danny's room ... had his dad done anything to it? What was he using it for now?

"Yeah, we, uh, all grew up here. We never lived anywhere else. This is a great old house," said Langley. "We think it was built in 1750, but Dr. Vaughn at the library thinks it's even older than that."

Langley suddenly knelt down. Delia was a bit startled, because she had no idea what he was going to do. He pulled back the throw rug.

"Look at these pine planks," said Langley. "Some of them are more than two feet wide. You can't even cut down trees that big any more. This is the original floor. This room, right here, was really the original house."

The original fireplace was still intact and in use, but the old beehive oven built into the wall next to the hearth wasn't used any more. Whenever Timothy Calhoun had a carpenter or an electrician or a plumber over to the house, he'd show them the beehive oven, and all of them, to a person, appreciated the craftsmanship and the beauty of the thing.

Langley picked up what looked like an old metal ladle. “The story goes that this thing has been hanging on the same hook in the same place for the past two hundred fifty years," he said.

"What is it?" Delia held it gently in her hands.

"They say it was a smelter. They'd use it to melt metal, make bullets, that sort of thing."

"That's really pretty cool," said Delia. "Now tell me about this." She was talking about the four walls of the living room which were not covered by wallpaper but were decorated by a painted mural that traveled from one corner to the next. The mural, more than a hundred years old, essentially told the story of how Fenton, or Oquossoc, began with the early settlers greeting the Indians, the building of the town's First Congregational Church, hunters hiding in the woods tracking deer, the first mill that was built along the banks of the Oquossoc. All of it was there in loving, if crumbling, detail.

Langley often heard the story that when his parents first looked at the house, it was an absolute shithole, but his mother saw beyond all that. Maureen Allen Calhoun especially loved that mural, and because she did, she had to have the house.

"Wouldn't you love to have heard what was talked about in this house?" said Delia.

"We used to talk about that, how they probably sat in front of the fire talking about the Revolution, Washington, Jefferson, the new Congress," said Langley.

"The Civil War, Lincoln," said Delia.

"Everything, everything," said Langley.

"What is your favorite memory here?"

It was a funny and unexpected question, but the strange thing was that Langley knew exactly what his favorite memory was.

He took Delia by the elbow and led her over to one of the front windows that looked out onto the street. "When I was about six or seven, my mother said, 'Langley, Danny, Brian, come here quick.' This was Christmas, and it was snowing, just how you would like it to snow at Christmas, and we went to the window. What we saw was Santa Claus, walking down the street, just as he was passing right below the streetlight. He was lit up by the light, and the snow was flying all around him. We watched Santa Claus walk right by the house. He was smoking a pipe."

Delia’s face expressed her joy.

"He walked right on by," said Langley, remembering how he had watched in silence as the old elf walked by the house. "He was wearing a tweed coat and a tie and a hat, and the white beard was blowing in the wind. I figured he must have only worn the red suit on Christmas Eve. We had actually seen Santa Claus. It was a miracle to believe in something like that." Langley's voice trailed off.

Delia and Langley were standing next to each other at the window. Their faces were at the same level so that when they turned to each other, they were staring into each other's eyes. They both leaned in silently and kissed.

Delia's mouth was soft and full, and Langley made sure that he actually felt it and remembered it. She opened her mouth just a bit and licked the end of his tongue. Langley put his hand on the side of her face, and Delia gripped the back of his neck with her open hand. She closed her eyes, and then she opened them to look into Langley's face.

As the kiss ended, Delia cupped Langley's mouth in her hand and kissed him again. They stopped and held their breath.

"Goddamn," said Delia. "It's about time." They both burst out laughing. "You are about the slowest moving bastard I ever met." And they laughed again.

"I ..."

"No, no, no," Delia was shaking her head with a smile on her face. "I'm just kidding. I ..."

She stopped short from saying what she had been about to say, but Langley knew what it was, and he wanted to say it, too. Instead, "It turned out that it was my father," was all he could think of saying, and they laughed again.

"Oh, man," said Delia, mock fanning herself. "What a fucking relief." They kissed again and held hands as Langley took her upstairs.

"This was my room," he said, opening a door. It was a dim place, filled with boxes and old clothes and some spare pieces of furniture that the old man didn't need any more.

Delia was gripping his hand. She had laced her fingers through his, and she was tightening her grip. Langley thought she was as nervous as he was.

He took her over to the window. "I used to look out this window, and I'd think of things like, I wonder what this street will look like when I graduate from high school? What will it look like the day I get married? What will be happening in the year 2001? I thought of the most fantastic things, and the thing of it is, this view hasn't changed one bit. The Gamminos' house—I still call it that, but they died years ago—is still white, the trees are still here. That old maple over there is never going to change. It hasn't really changed at all, not at all."

They went down the hall to what had been Danny's and Brian's room. Langley hesitated as he put his hand on the latch. Delia put her hand on his, and Langley lifted the latch. The door sprung free, but he didn't open it.

"Oh, Christ," said Langley.

"It's going to be fine," said Delia.

"I ..."

"Let's do this now, please," she said. Her face was pleading, and there were tears gathering underneath her eyes.

Langley pushed the door open. He didn't hear the screaming. He heard the voices of Danny and Brian as young children. "Langley, let's go!" said Danny. Langley was shaking. He wanted to break free from Delia's hand. He yanked on it lightly, but she held tight.

The bunk bed was still there without its mattresses, just an empty frame with slats. The rest of the room was bare. Nothing. Langley didn't know if this was a relief or if it terrified him. *Why wouldn't you hold on to things that were sacred,* he thought? *But how can you hold onto anything that's sacred?*

"Oh, goddamn it," said Langley. His breath left him as though he had fallen and the wind had been knocked out of him, and he was crying now. He balled his hand up into a fist to try to gather his strength and keep from crying any more.

"It's OK, it's OK, it's OK," said Delia. "I'm right here."

"I have a couple of things of Danny's. Little toys, things like that. A bandanna he used to wear," said Langley as they drifted to the center of the room. "You have to keep something."

He was taking in short, quick breaths. He put his hand over his mouth. He kept pulling in air through his nose, which was running, and his eyes fluttered because they were stinging from the salt in his tears.

"Goddamn it all to hell," he said through his sobs. He looked to the ceiling, and then he shook his head violently as though he was trying to shake everything off. They stood there for a few minutes. Delia pushed her body up against Langley's as close as it would go. The sobs stopped. He let out a deep breath of relief, and he wiped his tears and swallowed.

"I'm OK," he said.

"I know it, I know it, Honey," said Delia, but her voice was just as unsteady.

On the windowsill were a cleaning rag and a bottle of Pine-Sol. When Langley picked up the rag, it was stiff, as though it had not been touched in years. At the bottom of the bottle of Pine-Sol was a layer of sediment.

"I haven't been in here at all since Danny died." He sighed. He pressed his fingers into his eyes to stop the tears. "You couldn't go near it right after he died."

"Were you afraid?"

"My mom was always in here. She would spend hours in here, just sitting on the bed. Danny slept on the bottom bunk, and she would rock back and forth with his pillow tucked up in her arms, and sometimes you could see she had put it over her face, and she was just breathing him in, I guess." His voice was steadier now.

"I can't imagine the pain she felt."

"So my dad stayed downstairs and drank and smoked, and Brian acted out, you know. He smashed things, stole things. He might have been by himself for a whole year after that. I don't think I saw him with anybody," Langley said. "I certainly couldn't go near him. I didn't go near anybody for that year myself."

"Oh, Langley." Langley squeezed his eyes shut. "What do you remember about Danny?" said Delia, but her voice was barely a whisper.

Langley remembered that there had been a bunch of balloons that sat in the corner of the room, long, long after they had deflated. The balloons were left over from a birthday party. They were sitting in the corner because Langley's mother thought the balloons had been blown up by Danny, and she thought each balloon held his breath inside. The balloons got smaller and smaller and became wrinkled, tear-drop shaped relics from a long ago time. He was going to tell Delia that story, but he couldn't tell the story. He was exhausted. That was enough for now.

He closed the door to the room. "Oh, man," he said, and they stopped for a moment in the hall. He took a deep breath and let it out.

"Do you still want to go to the parade?" said Delia.

"Oh, yeah, yes," said Langley. He smiled as he looked at Delia. "Those ghosts and goblins got nothing on me."

Delia wrapped both her arms around one of Langley's, and they left the house together.

Forty

2:30 p.m. Main Street formed the entire route of the parade. It was only about a mile long. In the town square you could find the Baxter Public Library, the Municipal Office Building, the Police Station, the Volunteer Fire Station and the Woodman Middle School.

The high school band members in their bright green and gold uniforms were getting anxious to start the parade. The band uniforms had a slight modification this year. After the school committee had recommended cutting the music program, Bill Plano subsidized the school band budget for two years, and now their uniforms were adorned with the A & J Fill & Gravel logo. It was a sign of the times.

The senior class president and vice president, both girls, would ride in their own car. There was a float put together by a group calling itself The Junkyard Band, which played instruments they had found at the town dump. And, of course, there were twenty of the big-headed puppets that would be walking among the crowd, handing out apples and maple sugar candy and other locally made stuff.

There was the Boy Scout troop—Troop 2, because it was the second troop to be formed in the state. Langley laughed a little bit at their uniforms. When he had walked in the parade as a Boy Scout, all the kids wore a full uniform, but now half the kids were in jeans and other forms of casual dress.

At about quarter to three the participants started to get in line. The crowds began to stand on the sidewalk. There were people who had come out with chairs, drinks and food, which Langley found funny because the whole thing didn't last an hour.

Langley saw Arch Trimble, who was in uniform, and another young patrolman, who had just joined the force. He saw Ted Darrow, the new chief. Langley put on his sweater, because when the breeze picked up and the sun went behind the clouds, it got cold.

Delia huddled next to him, and Langley's father and Vance had staked out a place right next to them with a couple of folding chairs. The band started to play. Clouds had rolled in, and it suddenly looked like rain. Everybody kept looking at the sky.

Langley saw Maria Tull carrying the huge, white plastic molar she brought to the parade every year. The members of the Board of Selectmen always marched in the parade, and no one ever knew why. People don't like to see politicians when they're trying to have a good time.

Delia had leaned into Langley. He was pressing her shoulder into his chest, and he put his arm around her, and she moved in closer still. She wrapped her arms around his waist. He looked down at her and smiled a little awkwardly. She smiled back, and he knew it was all right.

Britney Sawuko, the reporter who had first written about the eagle, was walking around with her notebook, and she was followed by a photographer. She waved when she saw Delia and the Langley and went over to them.

"Hey, Chief," she said.

"Britney, how are you?"

"And Delia, right? You're the ranger?"

"Yes," said Delia, reaching out a gloved hand. "Good memory."

"Well, that was a good story. Can I get a quote for the paper, Chief?"

"About the eagle? No, no thanks."

"No, no, I'm doing a feature about the parade."

"Oh, sure, yeah, but you should really talk to my brother, he's Sam Hain."

"I talked to him already."

"What do you need?"

"Tell me how much you like the parade."

"It's great," Langley said and stopped. Britney stopped writing and looked up. "Chief, I need a little more than that."

"Oh, OK." He looked out over the proceedings and spoke in his on-the-record voice. "I think the Parade of the Horribles is one of the terrific things that make Fenton unique, a great place to live. Every year the whole town comes out to enjoy this family event, and it couldn't be more wonderful."

Britney was writing it down. When she was finished, she said, "Spoken like a true professional."

"That's what I used to be."

"See you around, Chief. Thanks." She looked at Delia. "Bye."

Down the road about a block away, Langley saw Bill Plano, who had his family with him, or so Langley presumed, and a couple of other people. When Plano saw Langley he waved and called him over.

"What do you think he wants?" Langley said to Delia.

"Don't go over to him. Just give him the finger."

"You mean the bird, right? I should give him the bird?"

"Yes, funny man," said Delia, "the bird."

But Plano was waving Langley to come over, and Langley said, "I'll be right back."

"Hey, Chief, I just wanted to introduce you to my family. This is my wife Chris, and this is Bill, Gene and Wally." He was introducing his children. "This man used to be the Chief of Police here."

Only one of the kids could manage a dispirited "cool" in response.

"How are you feeling?" asked Plano.

"Fine, completely healed. I mean, what's left of my shoulder is completely healed," said Langley.

"That must have been a terrible thing to go through," said Chris Plano.

"It was pretty bad," said Langley.

"I understand you're kind of looking into this bird business again." *Ah, here we go,* thought Langley. "I just want to say that if there is anything we can do, please ask, and the reward money still stands. God knows I hate to cash a check if I don't have to, but this one I'll be happy to." Plano's two sycophants laughed emptily at the tired joke.

"I'll be sure to let you know, thanks," said Langley. He was going to say he had all but dropped the entire thing, but he let it go.

"Hey, the band uniforms look great, don't they?" said Plano.

"They sure do," said Langley. "Well, listen, I have to get back to my family. It was nice to meet all of you."

"OK, chief, and remember what I said," said Plano.

"I will," said Langley.

Antonio Meli was standing next to Delia when Langley cut back across the street.

"Consorting with the enemy, I see," said Antonio.

The band was playing and leading the procession as it slowly made its way up Main Street. The band was followed by the selectmen and then by a float sponsored by Tull's Family Dentistry, which had kids on it flinging out sugar free candies to the people on the side of the street.

They were followed by The Junkyard Band and then the town's Little League teams. Right after that came the Boy Scouts and the Cub Scouts. As the Cub Scout den walked by, Antonio, Langley and Delia quietly looked at each other.

The five members of the den were wearing Indian headdresses adorned with exotic bird feathers. The feathers were clearly real, and the headdresses were handmade. The kids were making whooping sounds. There were dozens of exotic feathers on the heads of the boys.

Delia snapped some photos, and they watched as the boys headed down the street. When Langley looked to find Bill Plano, he could see that Plano was taking pictures of those kids, too.

Forty-One

Sunday, October 31. Langley and Delia were standing in Langley's old office with Chief Darrow. They were looking at the photos Delia had taken.

"Well, they do look pretty unusual," said the new Chief.

"We just need to ask where they got them," said Langley.

"Do you know the name of the den leader?"

"It's Red Richardson's daughter."

"All right," said the new chief, sighing a very deep sigh. "Let's go."

When Martha Richardson Clark answered the door, she clearly looked alarmed. "Chief," she said to Langley, and then she nodded to Darrow. "What can I do for you?"

Chief Darrow spoke up. "I wanted to ask you a quick question, Mrs. Clark. No one is in trouble, there's no problem with the law here, but I do have a question I need to ask." His voice was very kind.

"That's a relief, but you've still made me nervous," she said.

"Do you think we could come in for a second?" asked the new chief.

"Of course." Mrs. Clark opened the door no wider than necessary to allow the two men in one at a time. She did not want them in her house, whether there was anybody in trouble or not. Mrs. Clark was divorced, so there was no husband home. They could hear the TV in the background. They stood awkwardly in the living room.

"Mrs. Clark, your Cub Scouts were wearing some unusual costumes at the parade."

"Yes," she said. The poor woman was clearly nervous. "I didn't see them until I saw the boys at the parade. They were keeping it a surprise." She knew where this was headed.

"Specifically, their feathers ..."

"Yes."

"I was wondering if you or your son knew where they came from."

She drew in a deep breath. "I actually don't know. Would you like to ask Cal?"

"Is Cal your son?"

"Yes."

"He's a member of the pack?"

"Yes."

"We'd like very much to talk to him, if we may. Please also ask him to bring his costume," Darrow said.

"Of course." She left the room, and Langley and the chief looked at each other. Darrow made a *we'll see* gesture. A small boy wearing the exact same worried look on his face as his mother's walked into the room holding onto his headdress. It was made out of a band of brown construction paper with the feathers glued and taped onto the outside of the band. Mrs. Clark had her arms around her son's shoulders.

"Cally, these gentlemen are from the police, and they have a question they need to ask you."

The new chief leaned over. "Cal, you're not in any trouble, but I do need some information that you may have, OK?"

The boy nodded.

"May I see this first?" Darrow pointed to the headdress. The boy handed him the costume. Darrow looked at it and then handed it to Langley. The feathers were worn and obviously not store bought. They were real. They were crumbling.

"I was wondering where you got those feathers from. If you have any information, this could be very helpful to us," Darrow said. His voice was very steady and kind.

The boy looked at his mother, then back at the policemen. He stood frozen for a full fifteen seconds.

"Cal, you're not in any trouble," said the mother.

"Where did you get the feathers?" asked Darrow.

"We rode our bikes up to the gravel pit." The boy's voice was shaky. Langley's hands were sweating.

"Which gravel pit?"

"The big one, the one where they bring the stuff in."

"The one right off 136?"

"That's right," said the boy.

"And you found the feathers there?"

"Yes."

"When did you find them?"

"Last spring." He turned to his mother. “Mom?"

"It's all right, Cal. It's fine," she said.

"What can you tell us about the feathers?"

"We used to go up there and just look through the junk, and then one day Aaron, he's my friend …"

"Aaron who?"

"Aaron Cote."

"OK," said the new chief. "It's OK. He's not in any trouble either. Go ahead."

"Aaron was going through a pile of junk, and there were all these feathers in a big mess," said Cal, "like a clump of them. They were all over the place. If you just looked around you could see them everywhere."

"What else did you find?"

"There were bottles and ..."

"No, I'm sorry, Cal. Did you find any other animal parts?"

"It was gross."

"So you did find other animals?"

"Yes."

"And what did you do when you found the feathers?"

"We looked around for as many as we could find, and we took the best ones. Then we said we'd be Indians for the parade."

"What did you do with the feathers after that?"

"Aaron kept them in a box at his house."

"Can you tell me again when you found them?"

"It was during school vacation."

"When?"

"Spring vacation, but it was Aaron that kept them in his house."

Darrow put on his hat. "You're sure about when you found them?"

"Why don't you ask the Cote boy?" said the mother.

"We will," said Darrow, "we will." He looked at Langley. "Thank you, both of you. Cal, you've been very adult and very helpful. We appreciate it. We're going to take this costume, OK? It would be a big help to us."

"Cally, you can go back now," said the mother. Cal quickly turned to get out of the room.

Langley spoke up. "Cal, I have just one more question." He turned to the mother. "I'm sorry. Just one more."

She sighed. She looked very unhappy.

"Chief?" Langley said, looking at Darrow, who nodded his permission. Langley stood directly in front of the boy. "Cal, I'm just wondering. Did you and your friends also find the strange-looking eagle that was in the news last spring? Do you remember that?"

The boy was really shaking now.

"Cal, please tell the chief if you know something, please!"

Cal blurted out, "It was dead when we found it! It was already dead! I swear! I swear!"

"I know it was, Cal." The rawness of the boy's emotions threw Langley. He didn't like to see it. He knew what it was like to be a terrified kid. "I understand, but you boys found that eagle, yes?"

"I didn't find it! Aaron did!"

"Where did Aaron find it?"

"He found it at the gravel pit with the feathers. It was already dead."

"I know, Cal. But what I want to ask you next is who … something was done to the bird after it had died. Do you know what I'm talking about?"

The boy's head was whiplashing back and forth between Langley and his mother.

"Did you boys do anything to the bird after it was dead?"

The boy was trembling, and he had gone completely white. Langley wasn't sure if the kid was going to vomit or not. He stood there trembling.

His mother leaned over and looked in her son's eyes. "Cally, did you have your Swiss Army knife on you that day?"

The boy was trembling so hard you could barely tell that he had nodded yes, but he nodded. His eyes were almost closed, and his mouth was clenched shut. His lips were white.

"And did you use that knife to cut the bird, Cally?" The boy's poor mother was shaking almost as violently as her son, but while the boy was just scared she was both scared and sad.

He nodded yes again.

"Cally, I need you to be very clear with me," said Langley. "What did you use the knife for?"

The boy turned to his mother and hugged her around her neck.

"Oh, my God! You know what happened, you have your information, now please!" She looked panicked.

"It's OK, Cal. Good job," said Langley. "Good job. It's OK, Cally. It's fine."

"Are the people who own the gravel pit dangerous people?" Martha Clark asked. "I've heard that they are."

"They're not going to hurt anybody, Mrs. Clark," said Darrow.

"Oh, my God," she said.

"Please don't say a word about this, please," said Darrow. "If you do, that could just complicate matters. I mean that."

"Oh, Jesus," the woman said and sank into the couch. Cal ran into the other room. "I can't afford this. Oh, my God." Her hands were shaking.

"Nothing's going to happen," said Darrow. "I want to thank you for taking the time to talk to us. I know this was … not welcome."

"I hope it wasn't a mistake," she said. When she looked up the tiredness and fatigue that must always be with her showed in full. Her eyes were puffy and red, and she looked ten years older than she had when Langley and Darrow knocked on her door.

When they were back in Darrow's car, Langley noticed the new chief looked somber, unhappy, but Langley didn't say anything. They drove in silence for a while, and Darrow's mouth was tight.

"Well," Darrow said as they neared the police station. "We're going to regroup on this thing first thing Monday morning."

"If there's anything I can do, let me know," Langley said. He was holding the little paper and feather headdress in his lap. "You may want to take this over to Delia. She'll know how to identify these feathers."

Darrow just nodded. He pulled up alongside Langley's car. Langley wanted to say something. He knew that Chief Darrow was thinking not only about how he was going to handle the crime, but also how he would deal with more press, more unhappiness, more political posturing. He would have to put up with a public debate about how he performed during the investigation. "Baptism by fire," he said as Langley got out of the car.

"You'll be all right," Langley said and knocked for luck on the side of the chief's car

Forty-Two

Monday, November 1, 7:00 a.m. But there was no time to regroup.

Two white vans with no markings made their way up Route 136. Antonio Meli happened to be driving back from the store when he saw them, and he watched the trucks make their way into the entrance of A & J Fill & Gravel.

When he got back to his house, he walked up the hill to the edge of his property, to the spot where he and Langley had first looked out over at the landfill last spring. He saw the vans park, and then a small team of men got out of the van with canisters strapped to their backs. They sprayed liquid over the surface of the landfill. Others followed and began to light small but intense fires all over the landfill. They were all wearing hazmat suits.

Smoke billowed up. The fires gave off heat. Antonio could smell the accelerant from where he stood. "What the hell?" He took out his phone and called Langley to tell him what he had seen and where he was.

Five minutes later Langley was speeding up 136. He soon could see the smoke from the fires. He pulled into the access road leading to the pit. Another car was right behind him, and then another turned in as well. When he came up to the edge of the landfill, he saw the white vans and the strange men walking over the surface of the landfill. Antonio walked over his old stone wall and crossed to where everyone was standing.

Flames and smoke were spreading out everywhere. There were small fires all over the landfill. Langley could feel the heat. Antonio came over. Then Darrow showed up, and soon Brian Calhoun pulled in. They all watched as the fires burned.

Maria Tull was there, as was Pete Fuller, the fire chief.

"What's going on?" Langley asked Brian.

"We have a fire permit. Don't worry, Chief," said Brian.

"I'm not worried. I was just wondering what was going on."

"Well, we know that kids have been playing up here, and really there's no way to stop that, and we also know they smoke up here," said Brian. "Mr. Plano very prudently decided to make sure there was no chance of any kind of material that would make anybody sick or, God forbid, create any kind of explosion up here."

"Explosion," said Langley.

"We're just checking for pockets of methane, propane, butane, you name it."

"When did you get the permit?"

"I think it was this morning, wasn't it, Chairman Tull?" said Brian.

"First thing," said Maria, who had the document in her hand.

"The town was very accommodating," said Brian.

"I don't need to see it," said Langley.

"I'm not sure I was showing it to you," said Maria,

"Rest assured, any organic matter up there, anything rotting or anything that shouldn't be up there will all be burned away and won't cause any health hazards or any harm," said Brian.

Maria had her arms folded across her chest and was smiling contentedly.

"You goddamn people," said Antonio. "You fucking pieces of shit people."

Brian just looked over and smiled. "You're just a vulgar, ugly ..."

"Come on, Antonio," said Langley.

"Go where, huh, chief? Go where?" said Antonio, his voice full of venom.

Langley had seen enough. He walked past Brian and Maria, the whole crowd, and went to his car. He didn't know what to say or do. For the first time in his life he wanted to leave Fenton. He wanted to get out.

For the first time he hated his little town.

Forty-Three

Tuesday, November 2, 7:30 a.m. The sun was streaming through the window of the small kitchen in Langley's house. The rays were bright and even though it was cold outside, the kitchen was bathed in warmth. It was a spring-like heat that spread out across the table. The slanting light made it possible to see the tiny beads of water that hung inside the curls of steam coming off their coffee and tea, and they could see minute pieces of dust float gently through the air.

They were quiet. Delia held her head back to catch the sun, and Langley could see every detail of her lovely face. He could see the lines that were just beginning to form at the corners of her eyes and mouth, and they only served to make her more beautiful. He could see the veins in her strong hands. Her eyes were clear and lovely. She had Elizabeth Taylor eyes with lavender-colored irises, soft and full of compassion. Finally, she looked at Langley. The clarity of her vision startled him, and he could do nothing but give her his full attention.

"We can move out of here," she said. "We can just go."

Langley looked out of the window. The sun was rising, and the light in the kitchen was getting softer. "Maybe. Maybe we should," he said, but his smile was sad. "I certainly feel like it."

They sat for a few more moments, and then suddenly they heard a car door slam right out in front of the house.

Langley got up and went into the living room and looked out the window. He saw Bill Plano walking up the front walkway.

"It's Bill Plano," he said.

"What?" said Delia, joining him. "What does he want?"

One of Plano's constant assistants had also gotten out of the car, but he did not walk with Plano up to the house. The guy had, in fact, leaned up against the side of Langley's car. Before Plano had a chance to knock, Langley swung open the front door.

"Please don't do that," he said to the guy leaning against the car. The man smirked a little, leisurely peeled himself off the car and straightened up.

"Do you have a minute?" Plano said to Langley, putting one foot on the stoop. No hello, but that wasn't surprising. Langley glared at Plano's flunky. "Just two minutes," said Plano.

Langley looked at Delia. "Why would you?" she said, but then she let go of Langley's hand and walked to her car. Delia was headed to work. She got in and said to Langley, "I'll call you in a little while."

She took off, and Langley and Plano walked around the corner of the house and sat on a little bench out in front of a small garden. Langley wasn't going to bring Plano into his house.

Plano looked straight ahead as he talked. "Can we come to some sort of agreement that this is over now?"

"What's over?" said Langley.

"Your peevish little examination into my business, because there is nothing to find. Not anymore." Langley shrugged his shoulders and waited for Plano to speak again. "Look, I'm just a small businessman."

Langley burst out laughing. He was laughing at the complicated, institutionalized American machinery that allowed Bill Plano even to say such a thing. He laughed at the massive, systemic, sanctioned corruption that goes on every day that allowed Bill Plano not only to say that, but possibly to believe it.

From the municipal boards that were too afraid or unsophisticated to stop powerful business interests, to the federal government, which as far as Langley was concerned had ground to a complete halt, to people like Maria Tull, who wanted to appease the power structure because it kept her life reasonably comfortable and made her feel more powerful, Langley was laughing at all of it. Corruption and graft were the only things that ran smoothly any more as far as he was concerned.

"I'll ignore that," said Plano, appearing to feel stung by Langley's laugh, "because if it isn't over, and I mean this, I'm going to begin to take this personally. I'll exploit every weakness the Calhoun family has, and the weaknesses of the Calhoun family are, let's face it, easy to exploit."

Langley sat up. He was going to say something but thought better of it. Instead, he just nodded. Plano was going to have his say, and Langley was going to let him say it.

"I'll just demolish all of you, your brother included."

Langley knew Plano would keep talking. These guys with egos always had to make sure they got their point across, and if they didn't think their words were landing like heavyweight punches, they got frustrated and talked too much. They had an anger and an ego that can never be appeased. So Langley just looked like he didn't quite understand the seriousness of what Plano was saying and let him keep talking.

"Let me tell you, your fuckin' brother has more for me to smash up than you. The arrangement your brother and I have is very delicate, but it's secure, you know what I mean?"

So that was it. Plano had something on Brian, but Langley knew that this play wouldn't work, because he resolved right then that there were going to be no more secrets in the Calhoun family. Plano didn't know it, but his threat was suddenly out of date.

Langley cocked his head toward Plano as though he hadn't quite heard what was being said. This infuriated Plano. "I feel good about the fact that you and your brother will do the right thing," said Plano, his voice tightening.

Langley didn't say anything. "Yes, sir, I feel good about that." Plano strained for a reaction, but Langley wasn't going to give him any satisfaction. "You should be just trying to make a nice life for you and your friend Delia," said Plano.

Langley wasn't even going to let the mention of Delia get a rise out of him. Plano had balled his hands into fists. His knuckles were white.

"Do the right thing," Plano said.

Yes, Langley was more determined than ever to do the right thing.

LANGLEY CALLED ED LUSTIG to tell him about his conversation with Bill Plano. Lustig told Langley the one thing he never understood about people when they got threatened was why they kept it a secret.

"Tell everyone!" said Lustig. "Protect yourself! Fuck that guy!"

So Langley was going to tell everyone, starting with his brother Brian, and he would also tell Chief Darrow and Maria Tull and maybe even Britney Sawuko over at the paper so she could keep it in her back pocket. He told Delia. "That bastard," she said.

Lustig then told Langley he had come across something strange. "I was about to call you," he said after Langley had told him about the threat.

"Ed, I don't need work right now," said Langley.

"I was Googling the Ramos case just to make sure there wasn't anything new out there, and I was using different combinations of words, Calhoun, lawyer, things like that, and I came across a news item that I think references your brother."

"He's in the news all the time."

"Up in Maine? Northern Maine?"

"I don't know anything about that."

"Let me find it here."

"Something to do with the Ramos case?" Langley was confused.

"The story was from a paper called *The Weekly Nor'Easter,* published way the hell up north in Maine, and it mentions that an attorney named Brian T. Calhoun from a firm named Bessy & Calhoun represented a truck driver who had crashed his truck on a back road in Maine."

It didn't sound like something that Brian would be involved in at all. "That's definitely my brother. In what town?"

"Fairfax," said Lustig.

Langley shook his head. "It was an accident involving a vehicle? One vehicle?"

"I'll email you the clip from the paper," said Lustig, "but the odd thing is, this guy was driving a dump truck for a company from Vermont, and he was three hundred miles away going in completely the wrong direction, and when they pried the driver out of the truck, they found almost eighty thousand dollars on him."

"Eighty grand?" said Langley. "Where?"

"In the truck. They were sawing him out, cutting out pieces of metal. They cut into this cash box, and eighty grand came flying out onto the street," said Lustig.

"Jesus," said Langley.

"So, anyway, I guess your brother went up there and represented this guy at his arraignment. That's a little strange," said Lustig. "I'll send you the clip."

"Yeah, I'd like to see that." For the first time Langley realized he had gotten in the habit of using his left hand when he held the phone. He didn't use his right hand anymore because of the discomfort it caused him when he lifted the phone to his ear. It was another reminder of just how things had changed in the past year.

"I'll shoot it over now."

"Yes, thanks. What was the name of the company that owned the truck?" Langley asked.

"It's in the story."

"OK, Ed, thanks. I appreciate it."

"If you need anything else, let me know."

They hung up, and even though Langley knew the email was coming from Ed, he Googled "Brian Calhoun Weekly Nor'Easter," and up popped the website for the little newspaper.

He found the edition from a couple of weeks before, and opened up the pdf. It was a low-tech online version of a small paper. *$80,000 Found in Box,* read the headline. The subhead was, *Driver Charged in Single-vehicle Accident.* Brian was clearly identified as an attorney from his law firm, Bessy & Calhoun, and the driver, Joel Crews, age twenty-five, was identified as an employee of Dickey Bros.

Langley knew this name, Dickey Bros. He opened the file of the names of the companies that had dropped off their materials at A & J Fill & Gravel. The third name on the list that Antonio had compiled was Dickey Bros.

Langley called Lustig back.

"Do you remember when we did a little surveillance on the clean-fill a little while back and recorded the names of the companies going in and out?" said Langley.

"You got a match," said Lustig.

"Dickey Bros. It was in and out of the landfill."

"Your brother was probably doing his client a favor," said Lustig.

"Eighty grand is an awful lot of money for a truck driver," said Langley.

"Follow the money," said Lustig.

LANGLEY HAD TOLD HIS FATHER he would meet him for coffee. They sat at an outdoor cafe, The Morning Buzzzz, that was on a side street just off the town center. It was quiet, and it was a lovely afternoon. Seagulls floated overhead and squealed. Langley had told his father about the dump truck and the money and Brian's involvement when they talked on the phone.

"Dad," Langley said. "There's been a lot going on." His father didn't say anything. He sipped his coffee. "I feel, I'm not sure how to say this, but so much has happened, and I know it's been a lot of trouble and a lot of stress, but this is something I have to see through. I came across it, I was given this, and I have to see it through," he said.

His father looked off in the distance. He tilted his head. "I, um, the thing that I have to do, son, the thing that I am going to do, is trust you," the old man said, "but I'm worried for my family."

"I guess I realize that this may cause some pain," said Langley, "but I'm not afraid of it."

"Well, I am," said his father. "If this only affected you, I wouldn't mind so much." He paused. "It's not even that I mind, it's just that we've been through so much. As a family. I mean, your mother ..."

"Don't do that, Dad."

"No, no, I wasn't going to make you feel guilty. I just meant that I'm still dealing with that. Listen, I love Vance, I really do, and I think she loves me, but I'm still dealing with your mother's death. It's with me every day." He sighed. "I think about your mom and Danny." Just saying the names made old Tim Calhoun burst into tears. "I think about Brian, too, and I worry about you." He wiped his eyes.

"I know, Dad."

"It's hard." He did not look at Langley when he said this.

"I know."

"When was the last time you visited Danny's grave?" the old man said.

"It's been a while."

"Well, goddamn it, get over there, then," Tim Calhoun said.

"I will. I will."

"You say that all the time."

"That's been ... there's a whole lifetime full of hurt over there, Dad."

The old man put his coffee cup to his lips. His hands were trembling. He suddenly started to pat his jacket down as though he were looking for something.

"What, did you lose something?" asked Langley.

"I was looking for my cigarettes."

"You gotta be fucking kidding me," said Langley.

"It's just a couple a day. It's nothing."

"Are you crazy?"

"It's helping me cope."

"You had a goddamn heart attack, Dad."

"I know. I know."

"Do me a favor and don't smoke around me. I started up again and quit, so I don't want to be around it."

"OK, OK.

"I bet Vance isn't too thrilled with that."

"Sshhhh. She doesn't know."

"Dad, it's not as though she can hear us."

"She knows everything."

The two sat there for a moment drinking their coffees. The old man put his hand on Langley's shoulder. "I'll tell you something. When I was getting out of the army, a senior officer, a guy by the name of Contreras, he asked me what I was going to do when I got out. I said I didn't know. Now this was a disciplined guy, a career guy, he probably knew exactly where he was headed, always. If you didn't know what you were going to do, he probably thought that was a sign of weakness. But I said I didn't know, and this guy says to me, follow your dream, don't be afraid to follow your dream. I thought this was pretty extraordinary coming from a military man."

His father paused, and Langley knew enough to just let him finish.

"So I did. I came here. I started a family. It was just what I wanted to do, and thank God I did it." He looked at his son. "So I understand the need for you to do what you feel you have to do. Even if it's something I wouldn't do myself, I get it." He smiled, but it was a sad smile. "I wish I didn't, but I do."

Forty-Four

Monday, November 8. Langley drove to Fairfax, Maine up Route 91 and stopped at the place where the Dickey Bros. truck had flipped over. He was looking at a picture he had printed out from *The Weekly Nor'Easter*. He stared at the spot, hoping that it would reveal some secret. He looked at the headshot of the driver. All Langley saw was a pleasant looking young man, somewhat uncomfortable, but that was understandable.

He read the story over and over, and he looked at Brian's name in print, regarding it, wondering why it was there, what it all meant. He figured that Brian was there to make sure the young driver didn't say anything. Brian would have the authority to keep everything under control.

When asked about the money at his arraignment, the driver simply said he didn't trust banks. He had been saving his money up for years and felt more comfortable when he had it with him. It was a story that millions of people could identify with today. People would think two things about the driver: *I don't blame him for not trusting the bank,* and *I wish I had eighty thousand in cash.*

Langley decided to drive over to the Fairfax Police Department, which he found housed in a trailer. Langley could only shake his head. These cops up here in these tiny towns were probably making twenty-eight thousand a year and were now dealing with a lot more than just the average drunk trying to drive home from the VFW. All the local people could afford to give them was a trailer.

Langley knew there were meth labs up here now, drugs brought in under good old-fashioned entrepreneurial vigor. Go where the product is needed and there isn't any competition. Give away the first batch for free, and you're in business. Go where the cops are stretched thin.

Langley guessed there were positions open in this police department just like there were in every other police department in poorer cities and towns. He just knew they had to be understaffed.

The cops up here—the cops in most places, including Fenton, New Hampshire—were unprepared for the onslaught of a new kind of criminal: one who didn't care about the area, was unafraid of trying to bribe you, and wouldn't hesitate to hurt you or your family if you didn't take the bribe. It was an awful thing.

There was snow on the ground, and a little path had been shoveled leading up to the front door. It was cold, and the path was slick. The snow had turned into dirty ice. Langley walked into the little office, which was worn down to its nub. The floor tiles were worn away, and equipment was stored in the corner.

"Can I help you?" A young officer had walked up to the counter and was looking at Langley.

"Yes, my name's Langley Calhoun, I'm a private investigator." He showed the young cop his identification. "I was also the Chief of Police down in Fenton, New Hampshire."

"Yes, sir," said the cop. His demeanor hadn't changed when Langley identified himself. He was simply being polite.

"I'm wondering if I can speak to either the chief or the officer who was on duty a few weeks ago when that dump truck overturned itself on 91. I think the driver was charged, and I'm just trying to find out a little bit about it."

"The guy with the money," said the cop.

"That's right," said Langley, "with the money."

"Officer Chadwick took that call," said the cop. He went over to the computer. "The chief's not in right now," he added as he sat down.

"Do you know what the driver was charged with?"

"I'm looking that up now. Officer Chadwick has the night shift tonight." He clicked his mouse a few times. Langley looked at the old desktop computer. It was covered with grime and stickers. He shook his head. "The driver said he was trying to avoid a deer." He read a little more. "He was charged with driving with a suspended license, second offense, and operating under the influence. The guy was zonked."

"Anything else?"

"He has a court date coming up, November 18 in Alfred."

"What does it say about the money?"

"Officer Chadwick asked him why he was carrying so much money, and he said he didn't trust banks."

"The lawyer is listed as Brian Calhoun?"

The officer read a little. "I have the name of the bail bondsman, but that's it."

"The trucker worked for a company in Vermont. Did he give any indication why he was all the way up here?"

"No, sir. It's not against the law to drive through the country."

"No, it isn't," said Langley.

"That's about all I've got," said the officer. "There's something odd, though. The truck has been impounded, but ..."

"But what?"

"Well, we don't have any reason to hold it. It says that someone is going to come and pick it up."

"You don't know who?" asked Langley.

"No, sir."

"I appreciate your time," said Langley. He left one of his cards and asked if the chief could call him when he had a moment.

Langley drove into Fairfax by Route 91 just to take a look at the town. There was a copy shop and a health food store. There was a used book store. There was a florist and a body shop and a post office. There were two or three law firms, as always. There was the municipal office building, which was old and built out of granite that was quite beautiful. There was a video rental place and a tattoo parlor. There were people walking on the streets. It looked like any small New England town. There was a narrow common dividing the two main roads in the center of town.

And then Langley stepped on his brakes.

Housed in what looked like an old movie theater, something that had been converted a long time ago, was a Dirty Books store sitting right in the middle of town. Langley shook his head.

Not two miles from where the Dickey Bros. truck rolled over, the one that had dropped off materials at A & J

Fill & Gravel and was carrying almost eighty thousand in cash, and right on the same road was a local branch of a Dirty Books store, the chain that the law offices of Bessy & Calhoun represented.

Langley got out of his car and walked into the store. There was a young woman behind the counter. "Hey," she said, and just for a second she looked as though she was about to say something to Langley, as though she thought she recognized him. But then she stopped and looked back down at her book.

She thought I was Brian, Langley thought to himself.

There was music playing, and a video was being shown on a monitor without sound. You didn't need sound. The shelves were filled with thousands of shiny, silvery DVDs, their blaring covers leaving nothing to the imagination. There were rows and rows of sex toys. It embarrassed Langley to be in the store. He was repulsed by the images but only because there was nothing beautiful about them. He didn't have any morality about it. They were simply ugly.

He walked up to the girl. "Have you seen Brian Calhoun lately?"

She lifted her head slowly. It was bright in the store, but her pupils were the size of dimes. "Who?"

"Brian Calhoun. I'm looking for him."

She closed her magazine. She was thinking very hard about what to say, and in the end she opted to say nothing. She simply shook her head no and went back to her reading.

When Langley left the store, he looked up into the Maine sun. He wanted the light from the sun to burn off the film of muck that seemed to attach itself to his skin when he was in the store. He looked into the blue sky and breathed in the cool, clean New England air.

Forty-Five

Thursday, November 11, 9:00 a.m. Langley carried a piece of paper with a name on it into the FBI offices at One Center Plaza, which was right in downtown Boston, and went up the elevator to Suite 420. He was looking for Assistant Special Agent in Charge Wayne Johannsson, and he knocked on the door.

The door to Johannsson's office opened, and Langley was greeted by a young man dressed in a nice suit. He had a warm smile.

"Mr. Calhoun?"

"Yes."

"Come in, please. I'm Agent Wayne Johannsson."

"Thanks for taking the time to see me."

Langley walked into the modest office. He sat in a squat wooden chair with a black leather seat and waited until Johannsson walked behind his desk and sat down. There was no air in the room. It seemed hermetically sealed and silent. It was bright, fluorescent. The agent tented his fingers.

Langley had decided he was going to start with the day Antonio found the eagle and trace the story from that moment on, and so he did. He told the story about finding the decapitated eagle and showed Johannsson some of the photos that Delia had taken. He showed him the press clippings and the toxicology report from the lab. He told about filing the endangered species report and talking with the biologist from the Fish & Wildlife Services. He talked about how everything went cold and why he left his job as Chief of Police in Fenton. He told him about his relationship with his brother and who his brother's clients were. He walked him through the case in Manchester and getting shot. He told him about who he was working for in Manchester.

Agent Johannsson simply nodded.

Langley then told him about the parade and showed him the photos of the kids wearing the headdresses made out of the bird feathers. He related the conversation that he and Chief Darrow had had with Mrs. Clark and her son Cal. He told him about how Bill Plano had obtained a permit for a controlled fire and how the surface of the landfill was burned and how his brother said that any organic material would be burned away and would not be a health hazard to any of the kids who trespassed on the property at night.

Johannsson was leaning forward slightly.

Langley then relayed his encounter with Bill Plano and what Plano had said about Brian, and then Brian's sudden and inexplicable appearance at a courthouse in northern Maine representing the Dickey Bros. truck driver who had eighty thousand in cash in his truck.

"I see," said Agent Johannsson.

Langley showed him a copy of the list that Antonio had compiled of the names of the businesses that were going in and out of the landfill, which included Dickey Bros.

"Why were you undertaking a surveillance of the landfill?" asked the agent.

"I wasn't. Mr. Meli was. He thought, and I thought as well, there was some connection between the dead eagle, which was rare and not from New England, and the landfill. I thought it was reasonable to think the landfill business was somehow involved in the trafficking of endangered animals, or maybe the animals that died on their way to wherever they were going were being dumped at the landfill. Maybe they simply dumped the carcasses there along with the concrete and other debris," said Langley.

"Is there anything else you might have for us?"

Langley handed over his own report from the Fenton Police Department on finding the dead eagle. He also had a DVD that had various news reports about when the eagle was initially found.

"My question to you is, do you know anything about this? Are you investigating this, or do you think there is anything here to investigate?" asked Langley.

The agent unfolded his fingers and took a brief look at the materials that Langley had put on his desk. He just leaned over them. He didn't touch them.

"Why did you impound the truck that rolled over in Fairfax, Maine?" Langley asked.

Johannsson cleared his throat and said quietly, "I have no comment on that."

"I think my brother is in trouble. I think he's being blackmailed, or he feels he's compromised and can't do anything about it. Would it be ... would you find any value, if that is true and if you are looking into any of this, would it be helpful to him if he came in here and, and cooperated with you? Would that be beneficial to you in any way?" Langley let out a deep breath. "To him in any way?"

"The information you have here is interesting, but ..."

"Do you know anything about this, or is it new to you?" Langley had no idea if he was corroborating evidence the FBI already had or telling them something they didn't know. He didn't know if he was helping his brother or hurting him.

"Mr. Calhoun, I can't say anything about that."

"You think that would be helpful?"

"Mr. Calhoun, you're putting yourself in a very vulnerable situation here. Please don't press this any further."

"You think it would be helpful to him, I mean in terms of whether he is in any legal jeopardy?"

"Mr. Calhoun, I can't say anything about that. The only thing I can say is that I would hope that Brian would have the, um, desire to come speak with us. He's an attorney. He should know what to do."

"Are these names known to you?" Langley asked. "Do you know about Plano, about Brian, or anything about the landfill or the animal trafficking that may be going through there?"

"The animal aspect of your story is handled through another agency. We don't handle that," said Johannsson.

"But it's all together," said Langley.

"Mr. Calhoun, what kind of conversations are you having with Brian?"

Langley sat back in his chair. "There's no reason to start to investigate me, Mr. Johannsson," said Langley.

The agent didn't say anything.

"I'm not having any conversations with him."

"As a former member of law enforcement, Mr. Calhoun, I can only say that if you do talk to your brother, it should be to urge him to do the right thing."

"Do you need these files?" Langley asked.

"No."

Langley stood and left the office.

WHEN HE GOT HOME, LANGLEY SAT with his arms crossed. It was an unusually guarded position for him. He was frowning. He kept shaking his head. His meeting had been maddeningly inconclusive.

"You did the right thing," said Delia.

"I don't know. I don't know."

"What did you expect the guy to say?" said Lustig, who had been waiting for Langley to return. "It was a fool's errand."

"I just know that Brian is going to go down hard."

"You called the guy and said you had some evidence he might be interested in seeing about the landfill, about Bill Plano and all that, and you end up asking the guy if he's investigating your brother, and you expect him ..."

"I know. I get it. I know."

"It's ridiculous," said Lustig.

"I know."

"What did your brother ever do to help you?" said Lustig.

Langley wanted to say that his brother had done very little to help him throughout his entire life. When they were teenagers they barely spoke. Brian never took Langley anywhere, never introduced him to his friends, never let him meet the girls he was hanging out with. Langley would always be in another room, listening to

Brian and his friends laugh and play. Langley would look out the window of his bedroom and watch Brian drive away on a date. Brian refused to be best man at Langley's wedding to Julia. No, Brian had never done anything to help Langley.

But Langley knew what others had forgotten, which was that Brian had lost a brother, too, when he was very young, and very likely his best friend. What people forget about twins is that they are two halves, really, and so it is fair to say that maybe Brian had never really felt whole since the day Danny died, and maybe he never knew how to compensate for that incompleteness. So, no, Brian never did do much for Langley, but that didn't mean that the depth of Brian's pain should be forgotten.

Even so, Langley had to follow through on this thing. He knew in the deepest part of his soul that his family was going to go through one more paroxysm of real pain, of real twisting anguish and agony, embarrassment and very possibly jail. *This is going to be an absolute nightmare,* Langley thought to himself, but he had to do it. If they went through this hell together, there might just be a chance that they could begin to be honest with each other for whatever time together they had left in their lives.

Forty-Six

Thursday, 3:00 p.m. Eileen answered the door. Brian was not home.

"Where did he go, do you know?" Langley asked her.

"He went over to your father's house," she said. Langley turned away, and Eileen shouted, "Langley!" after him, but he kept moving. He knew that she would call Brian, but at this point it didn't matter. He didn't want to play out this drama in front of his father, but that didn't matter anymore either.

Langley pulled into Tim Calhoun's driveway and parked underneath the old maple. Brian's car was there. Langley half expected Brian to come out of the house to avoid a scene, but then again, maybe Brian would be more than happy to have Langley make a fool of himself in front of their father.

Langley walked through the screen door on the porch, then through the front door to the living room. The old man and Brian were sitting, having a cup of coffee.

"Langley," his father said, but it wasn't a greeting. He stood.

"Dad, I'm sorry, but I'm here to talk to Brian. Brian, we have to talk. Right now."

"Langley, what's happened?" said their father.

"You went over to the house and scared Eileen half to death. She just called. What's going on?" said Brian.

"Langley!" shouted their father.

"Brian, you know exactly what this is all about," said Langley, ignoring his father.

Brian sat down.

"Langley, what is going on?" said Tim Calhoun.

"Dad," said Brian, "you know how Langley ..."

"Brian, cut out the bullshit," said Langley, but he didn't raise his voice.

"Langley, tell me what's happened," said their father.

"Yes, what is it, Langley?" said Brian.

"I got a visit the other day from Bill Plano. He came to my house, walked up to me on my lawn with Delia right there, and threatened me by telling me that all this business with Antonio and the landfill and everything else had better be over."

"That seems reasonable," said Brian. "You've been harassing him ..."

"Stop," said Langley.

"... harassing him for the better part of a year. It doesn't sound like a threat."

"He said I had better promise him that it was over or, and this is what he said, he would exploit the weaknesses of the Calhoun family."

"What the hell did he mean by that?" asked Tim Calhoun.

"He said there were many weaknesses to exploit, particularly yours, Brian."

"Mine?"

"He said he was going to smash us up, and he would particularly enjoy doing it to you because you had more things for him to destroy than anyone else."

"He's just saying, Langley ..."

"Let me tell you something, Brian," said Langley, who didn't break a sweat. "Don't give me one of your legal explanations for something that was clearly a threat."

"Langley, sit down," said Timothy Calhoun.

"If I know anything, it's that if Bill has anything to use he'll use it. Now he doesn't have anything on me, and he doesn't have anything on Dad, but he called the relationship between the two of you delicate. Now what does he mean, and what is he going to do?"

"Langley, he was just using me to make a point. This is a businessman who has been forced to pay a lot of money out of pocket to keep his reputation intact because of an investigation headed up by you that never had to happen."

Langley shook his head. "This is a businessman whose business is so foul and corrupt that he has to spend a lot of money to keep people from looking into it," said Langley. "He's not protecting a good reputation. He's ensuring that the truth will never come out, and you're right in it."

Langley took a step closer. His father stood up.

"Why did you represent that truck driver from Dickey Bros. who had eighty thousand dollars in his truck? The guy who flipped his truck over a mile outside Fairfax where there is a Dirty Books store?" asked Langley. "What was he doing up there? What were you doing up there?"

Brian looked up in surprise.

"How much money is being laundered through A & J Fill & Gravel and Dirty Books?"

"Brian, what's going on?" said Tim Calhoun.

"I'll tell you who I think knows all about this, and that's the FBI," said Langley.

"The FBI?"

"Now, what is it, Brian? Can Plano blackmail you, or has he already been blackmailing you, because let me tell you something." Langley took a deep breath. "If he is, and we don't make the first move on this, he'll crush us. I'll be implicated. You'll go to jail."

Brian looked up, "Why did you bring up the FBI?"

"I went to them this morning."

"What did you tell them?"

"I told them everything I know. Brian, I've been threatened, our family has been threatened. Delia. I bet Eileen and the kids aren't far behind."

"Oh, Jesus, what have you done?" said Brian. His voice was full of real fear.

Tim sat next to Brian and put his hand on his son's shoulder. "Son," was all he said.

Langley took a step back.

"My boy," the father said with such sadness that Langley felt his body give way, as though he suddenly wanted to stop the whole thing. He wanted to shout out, "Let it go! Let it go!" but he didn't.

"Langley's right," said the father. "What do you know? What can you tell us?"

Brian stared into his hands. He looked up at Langley and said fiercely, "You can't do this."

"Brian, Brian," said the father. "Langley's telling you, but I'm asking you. What is it that he's saying? What did Mr. Plano mean? What can he do?"

There was a long, dreadful silence.

"Brian, go to the FBI. Cut a deal with them. Don't let them take control of this. Protect yourself," said Langley.

Brian Calhoun took in a deep breath. Then the three of them were silent. The only sounds were the occasional car traveling by the house, the clock ticking in the living room, and the hum of the appliances in the kitchen.

Tim remained sitting next to Brian. Langley sat in a chair across the room. The time crept by until the shadows got a little longer. Brian's phone rang. He took it out of his pocket and looked at the number.

"It's Eileen," he said softly. He put the phone back into his pocket. Tim looked over at Langley, but Langley sat expressionless. He felt bad for his father.

Another fifteen minutes passed, a quarter-hour of silence. Tim said, "Brian."

"There are things," said Brian, "that I should probably tell." His father rubbed his back. "You can imagine," Brian went on, his voice guttural, brutal, "there's a lot more money than people realize."

"What are you mixed up in," said the father.

"I simply did Bill Plano a favor a long time ago, that's what I had been asked to do, and then I was in it, couldn't get out of it. That was it. That was five years ago, and it all started with a simple, small favor that turned out not to be so innocuous after all," Brian said. He smiled in defeat.

"How do you think it's going to look that I was the goddamn chief of police while this was going on?"

"Langley," said the father in despair.

"I knew exactly how it was going to look," said Brian.

Langley let out a deep breath. "We're all in it," he said.

There was silence in the room. The breeze blew through the empty branches of the old maple out front, but nobody was really listening. It was getting dark now.

"Son, how did you expect to find your way out of all this?" asked the father.

Brian looked around the room. "More or less like this," he said.

Forty-Seven

Friday, 8:00 a.m. The next day the FBI raided Brian Calhoun's law office and the offices of A & J Fill & Gravel. They also raided the Dirty Books store in Salmon Falls.

They raided Brian's house and took his computers and files. They raided Bill Plano's house. They left Langley alone.

Agents from U.S. Fish & Wildlife arrived at other landfills owned by A & J in the region and the country. The news made national and international headlines.

Langley figured the FBI had to move fast because of everything that had happened. They had to act before everyone had a chance to do more covering up. They had to move before Langley tipped off Brian.

Brian and Bill were arrested on money laundering charges and mail fraud. They posted bail and tried to avoid the media.

Langley called Brian and urged him again to strike a deal with the FBI right away. "Bill Plano is not your friend," said Langley. "It's going to hurt, but you've got to do it."

It turned out that that FBI got some much needed luck when the truck turned over in Fairfax. They impounded the vehicle to get hold of the GPS system and the toll transponder attached to the windshield. Through both systems investigators were able to piece together the driver's route from when he left A & J Fill & Gravel through his stops at various Dirty Books locations in five separate cities.

The driver struck a deal and confessed that he had been picking up cash at A & J Fill & Gravel. The cash was paid by the animal traffickers to A & J so that some of the carcasses could be dumped there. The cash was given to some of the drivers that came in and out of the landfill, who were paid to drop the cash off at various Dirty Books store locations. The cash was then recorded as income from the franchise.

The driver of the impounded truck had been dropping off the eighty thousand dollars they had found in the truck when it rolled over. He told the agents that he knew it was no good, but he made some much needed extra cash making the deliveries. He had young kids. When asked who told him to pick up the cash, he said it was Bill Plano.

Plano denied it.

The truck driver told the press, "I'm not going to take the fall for a rich guy."

According to the news, a federal grand jury took less than two hours to indict Bill Plano and Brian Calhoun on felony charges. There were multiple charges against each of them. Brian was going to be brought before the bar.

The local cops went in to the Dirty Books franchise in Salmon Falls and boarded up the basement, which was a series of small rooms with holes in the particle board. The new store in Fenton never opened.

The landfill was shut down. Martin Poll, the biologist from Fish & Wildlife, went there one day to see if he could find any evidence of animal DNA that might support even more charges against Plano and Brian Calhoun. He and Langley and Chief Darrow and Antonio turned over the rock and concrete rubble, looking for evidence that there was a crime far greater than just money laundering committed at the landfill, but they did not find anything.

Subpoenas were issued to the companies that had dropped off their debris at the A & J Fill & Gravel landfill.

Forty-Eight

5:00 p.m. Ed Lustig handed Langley a drink.

"There is one thing I know about money laundering, and that's if you're going to do it, innocent people have to be recruited. People who in a million years wouldn't get involved have to do it," said Lustig. "You have to pay them off."

Ed was in full voice, drinking a scotch, smoking a cigarette, invigorated by the prospect of doing anything other than what he was supposed to do.

"There's no way around it," he said. "You have to take dirty money here, and you have to clean it over there. You can only do that by setting up corporations, you have to get banks to cooperate. There are an awful lot of people involved who need to keep their mouths shut. Sooner or later, something goes bump, and things unravel."

Langley was staring into his scotch. He didn't feel like drinking it, but he wanted to keep Ed company. His shoulder hurt, too, and his arm was feeling stiff.

"You'd think ..." Langley started to say, but he stopped.

"You'd think what?" said Ed Lustig.

"I was going to say something stupid," Langley said.

"Say it. I say stupid things all the time."

"I was going to say that you'd think people would just start doing the right thing," Langley said.

"I'm surprised that anyone in this late day and age does the right thing at all," Lustig said. "People think the world is dying, there's no tomorrow, their money isn't worth anything, and the fish are going away. So there is more graft and corruption, more outright criminality, than ever before. People are going to take what they want now. I'm not even sure people are worried about leaving anything decent for their kids. I'm not sure anyone's looking beyond the end of business today."

"I don't know," said Langley.

Lustig sat next to Langley and patted his knee. "But it really was a pretty good plan," he said. "People pay off Plano so they can dump prohibited materials, dump poached animals that have died, and give safe haven to the live animals that are on their way to someplace else. They drop the payoff at a pornographic book store. It's perfect. Who actually tracks the sales of pornographic materials? They just deposited a helluva lot more than what they actually took in."

Lustig was smiling as if he had solved the puzzle all by himself. "No one cares until an old man and a fired cop start to nose around, trying to find out what killed a strange looking bird," he said.

He poured himself a new glass and tipped the bottle toward Langley to ask if he wanted another drink, but Langley shook him off. "Jesus Christ, did you ever imagine finding that eagle would have amounted to all this? I mean, if you think about it ..."

"Oh, I've thought about it," said Langley.

Lustig smiled. "I know you have, but when you think about all the stuff that's happened because you and that old man followed through on that, it's amazing."

Langley simply nodded.

"I mean, even you getting fired was something of a result of all that."

"You bet it was," said Langley.

"And everything after that," Lustig said.

"Even Delia."

"Especially Delia," Ed said, clinking glasses with Langley. "That's right." They sat silently for a moment, taking it all in. "Incredible. Did you ever have any idea?"

Langley didn't say anything.

"One little bird," Lustig said, finishing his glass.

"That's right," said Langley, finally taking a big gulp of his scotch, "one goddamn little bird."

Forty-Nine

In Fenton, reaction to the situation was mixed. On Fentonville.com, people wondered who would help fund the high school band, who had the money to maintain the public pool, and how the tax base would be affected if A & J Fill & Gravel shut down for good. People worried about their property taxes going up, and those who were most concerned about that heaped scorn on Langley.

Langley read the comments online. He didn't recognize the reckless egomaniac that some people made him out to be. His detractors were few, but they were vocal.

He was compared to the trash that was dumped at the landfill. He was compared to a bird with clipped wings. There were some thoughtless allusions to decapitation. People posted drawings and pictures that had been altered. In one, Brian was a big fat bird sitting on a big fat egg that was supposed to represent the earnings he had made through the years of representing Bill Plano and the Dirty Books franchise.

Langley's family was being chewed up, picked apart, shredded. He was, however, a hero to many more. There was a small movement to bring him back as Chief, but that didn't go anywhere, and besides, people liked the new chief. Antonio wrote on Fentonville.com that Langley should run for selectman.

Some people were tasteless enough to bring in Danny and their late mother and to question what may have happened inside the Calhoun family to have caused all this wreckage.

One night Delia caught him sitting in front of the computer, his face glowing from the light of the screen. She sat down next to him. "What are you doing?"

He just shook his head.

"You don't have to know what people are saying any more," she said. Langley still hadn't completely realized that his future didn't hinge on what people in town thought of him. He really didn't have to worry about that any longer.

Delia shut off the computer, took him by the hand, and led him to bed.

ALMOST EVERYONE IN TOWN came to the painful realization that there was little, if any, difference between the networks' coverage of the story and the tabloids' coverage

Fenton was portrayed as a hotbed of corruption, a place where greed and larceny ran rampant. Langley and Brian were described as small town versions of John and Robert Kennedy, creating and enforcing laws that benefitted no one but themselves. Magazine writers, novelists, and freelance reporters all started to come through Fenton, wanting to write about how this one small New England town had changed.

"How can you know how we've changed if you don't know what we were like before?" Antonio asked one reporter who was trying to interview Langley and him one day at the diner. "What's different?"

"Are you saying that Fenton has always been this corrupt?" asked the reporter.

Antonio extended his forefinger and pressed the tip of it right in the middle of the reporter's forehead—a move that Langley had never seen before in his life—and pushed the guy's head back.

"You," said Antonio to the reporter, "can go fuck yourself."

A movie producer called Langley and said he was interested in filming the story of a small town police chief who brings down his own brother. "That's not what ..." Langley tried to say, but the producer kept on talking.

Antonio stopped speaking to everyone because he was continually asked his opinion of the Calhouns.

What had been lost in all of this was the eagle.

"Are you looking into what a problem all this animal poaching is?" Antonio asked. Langley, too, tried to remind the reporters about the eagle, but no one cared about the bird.

FBI Special Agent Wayne Johannsson reminded Langley that the animal trafficking was not part of his investigation. "But if it was going on," said Johannson, "it's been stopped."

Langley drove down to the United States District Court in Boston the day of Bill Plano's arraignment. He wanted to see Plano stand in the dock in front of the judge. Langley pictured Plano defiant and unbowed. What he really wanted to see was a broken man, but he knew he would be disappointed.

At 10:00 a.m., Plano and his lawyers filed into the courtroom. The judge walked in, everybody stood. The case, *United States v. Spiral Enterprises (2011),* was read aloud, and the judge asked the defendant how he intended to plea. In a clear, ringing voice, Plano said, "Not guilty."

His bail was set, his passport was revoked, the terms of his release were read, and the date of the trial was scheduled. He was not to leave Fenton.

Everybody related to the case cleared out of the room. Langley sat for a moment. He closed his little notebook, but he hadn't taken any notes. He got up and left and was walking down the steps of the courthouse when he saw Plano get into the back of a huge SUV. Plano didn't look smaller, he didn't look diminished, but that would all change somewhat months later when he and Brian would plead to much lesser charges, and Plano would be sentenced to eighteen months in federal prison and Brian to six months.

In the meantime, Timothy Calhoun was pleading with his children to continue to speak to each other, to talk, to get through this thing as best they could.

Fifty

Friday, November 16, 4:00 p.m. Langley and Brian were sitting at a table on the sidewalk in front of The Morning Buzzzz. It was biting cold, and Brian was smoking. The two of them sat at opposite sides of the table. Brian was looking at the dirty sidewalk.

"I smoke too much," said Brian.

"I had started again," said Langley.

"Have one."

"No, thanks, I stopped again too."

"You started and stopped?"

"I got shot," said Langley.

"That'll do it," said Brian. He had a habit of squeezing the coal at the end of the cigarette onto the ground and then putting the butt into his coat pocket. This is what he did now. It was what their father used to do.

"I've been meaning to ask you about the kids," said Langley. "How're they doing?"

"We took them out of school," said Brian.

"Oh, Jesus," said Langley. "Are they home?"

"They're at Nova's," Brian said.

"Vermont? Eileen's sister?"

Brian nodded. "I never did understand that name. How do you name one kid Eileen and the next kid Nova?" Brian took out another cigarette and put it between his lips. "Does this bother you?" The cigarette bounced up and down when Brian spoke.

Langley shook his head. “I like the smell of it.”

After a moment Brian said, “We’re going there for Thanksgiving, by the way.”

“I guess I’ll have dinner with Delia at her apartment, or we’ll ...” Langley sighed. “I don’t know.”

“How’s that going?” Brian lit the cigarette and inhaled the smoke as deeply as Langley had ever seen anyone inhale cigarette smoke. Brian’s chest puffed up and then he let the smoke out in a massive plume. The sight was both impressive and frightening.

“I just feel as though I fell into this lucky thing. It’s been incredibly ... I just feel incredibly lucky,” said Langley.

“I mean, Julia was lovely and all, but …” said Brian.

“Julia and I never had a chance. We just, I was just … I couldn’t ...”

Brian said, “I know.”

“I guess I’d better go over and see dad. Are you going to come?”

Brian shook his head. “I think Vance has pretty much moved in.”

“Good.”

“She makes the old man happy,” said Brian.

“We need to keep talking,” Langley said suddenly. “We just need to keep talking through this whole thing.”

They sat silently for a minute.

“Yeah,” said Brian. “This was really good.”

Fifty-One

Delia was waiting for Langley at the Postwar Villa. Her thick red hair was down, and a smile was on her freckled face when she opened the door. She hugged him silently and looked him intently in the eyes.

"What is it you'd most like to do?" She lifted herself up and kissed Langley softly.

"Take a walk, maybe, walk around town." He sighed.

"Good," said Delia.

Langley wanted to walk through his town to take a look at it because he felt he was going on a long journey away from it. He didn't feel melancholy. He simply wanted to gather up some memories and images of the place. He felt like he was moving away, but he didn't know why he felt that way.

Delia and Langley left the house and walked into the center of town.

There was a small half-shell stage on Lara Bricker Park, where the schools and the town held concerts and summer festivals and had the Memorial Day speeches. An old man in purple shorts sat on a stone wall smoking a cigarette looking out over the Oquossoc.

They walked down Main Street and past the library. The library was showing a series of Hitchcock films, and someone had made a mistake and scheduled a movie, according to the sign, called *The Bird with the Crystal*

Plumage, which may have been a lot of things, but it definitely wasn't Hitchcock.

Of course, there are things you see when you walk that you don't when you drive. Langley realized he had not walked through town in years, maybe not since he had been a kid. He saw Mrs. Agran watering her lawn.

On Portland Street they walked by a wooded section that was deeper and darker than Langley remembered. There was a deep gully running through the middle of it. It might have been an old brook, and the ground around it was strewn with junk. Pieces of PVC piping, old coolers, and a few tires littered the ground. There were a few old bull pines with limbs that twisted and turned in their efforts to find some sun. Half the branches had been amputated.

Langley remembered that when they were kids, he and Brian and Danny had picked up sticks and spent hours smacking the low, dead branches off the pines.

They looked at the tiny family graveyards tucked away in corners all through town. They walked by a lone unmarked headstone just off the traffic circle. That headstone had to be more than a hundred years old, but there was no name etched into the granite. Years ago, many years ago, someone had said it was put there for the unnamed dead who came back from the wars, but no one ever really knew. No one knew who put it there. No one wanted to remove the stone, either.

As they walked, Langley looked down on the pavement, and he saw the remnants of trash that had fallen out of cars. There were pieces of shoelaces. There were pennies, bottle caps, soda bottles and beer cans. There was the sand left over from winter. There were shards of garden pots. There was a baby bottle nipple and the fragment of a page from a Victoria's Secret catalogue. Anything and everything that people carry in their cars that they want to get rid of, or that gets scattered when there is a crash, was there. All of it was littered along the sides of the roads in Fenton.

Acorns that had fallen onto the sidewalk crunched beneath their feet.

He looked at the houses. The new houses, seemingly made of plastic and buckling Plexiglas, already looked old and saggy. The older homes, so eloquently placed in the land, stood tall and straight and retained their right angles. Langley disliked the newer homes intensely. They were homes that looked like they could have been built anywhere. *This is New England,* Langley thought, *it should look like New England.*

Antonio had a phrase for architecture that belonged to a certain region: vernacular architecture. There was none of that.

Delia hugged him around the waist and pulled him in close. They walked toward Leonard's Hill.

Langley felt happy, but every time he felt that way his mind wandered back to the day Danny fell out of that tree. He knew it was a trick his mind used to stop himself from feeling too good, from being too happy. After all, how could he be happy after what he had done to Danny? Memories were floating all around him now.

He thought of Danny climbing up that tree and wondered what would have happened if they had been called down by their parents, or the weather had been bad that day, or they had decided to stay inside, or … to infinity.

The whole thing had such a feeling of inevitability about it, as though they had been hurtling toward that day and that moment, and there was nothing that could have ever prevented or changed what happened. It was as though Danny had been meant to die at that moment since the day he was born.

Stop it, Langley said to himself. *Stop*. They kept walking, and he knew Delia could feel his body tensing up.

Even their father cutting down that tree never changed it. He had savagely cut down that pine, cut it and chopped it out of existence, but it never changed anything. Since the day Danny fell out of that tree, Langley simply believed that terrible things would always happen to him.

A sharp yelp, a sharp snap, and screaming.

Stop it. He shook his head.

"What?" said Delia.

He had heard that screaming in his head for thirty years now. He had heard Danny's screams every day for thousands and thousands of days. He had heard his own screaming in the middle of the night, and sometimes during the day, more times than he would care to count. He was tired, exhausted, spent, withered from hearing those screams.

As he aged the tragedy seemed to weigh on him more and more. It did not lessen with each passing season, and he wondered if his brother and father felt the same way. He wondered if it had eventually killed his mother, if the cancer that had killed her was the result of the intensity of the tragedy that she kept inside herself.

"What is it?" said Delia. He wanted to tell her. He wanted to.

"Oh, Honey," she said so sadly, so mournfully, that Langley knew she was saying, "I want you to feel better. I want you to be happy. How can I make you happy?"

For years and years he had wanted to keep the sharpness of the pain of Danny's death close at hand. It was Langley's penance, his duty, the process that allowed him never to forget. It was something he felt he had to do. He deserved Brian's wrath and scorn, didn't he? But how wasteful that had been.

"Please tell me something good," Delia said.

Now it was time, more than time, to let the pain go and let more of the happier memories in, to treat Danny with respect. Danny had been alive.

"Langley, hey, Langley." Delia was trying to bring him back. "I don't want to lose you any more, OK? Stay with me." She held his face. Her green eyes were sharp and alive when she spoke, and Langley could see the hundreds of freckles that made her face seem so ... what was the word he was looking for? They made her face dance, but it was more than that.

She was smiling at him, and he looked into her eyes. "Please," she said.

"It was," Langley said, shuddering deeply, "an accident."

"Yes, yes, Honey. I know. I know. I know. It was an accident. Yes." She looked searchingly at him, her eyes pushing him to say something else.

There were things that he held inside that he wanted to give to her willingly. He was searching inside his mind, and he thought of a moment when he and his brothers were all together. He remembered a time, one day during the fall a long time ago, and he wanted to tell Delia all about it.

"Langley?"

Langley opened his eyes and looked at Delia. Her face was dancing.

"Tell me," she said.

Something jumped up from his abdomen and into his throat and right up to his eyes. He blinked for a few moments and was surprised at the power these words seem to carry. The two of them stood at the top of Leonard's Hill. *Tell her.*

Langley pictured himself climbing up Leonard's Hill with Brian and Danny. They all reached the top of the hill, and the sun was going down, and they were standing in a line at the top of the hill with Brian holding onto the handle of their wagon. This was the moment he wanted to tell Delia all about.

"Let's go!" Langley could hear Danny's voice now. He and Delia stood in a gentle breeze, just standing next to each other, looking down at the familiar slope of Leonard's Hill, with the leaves rolling over the pavement.

"Come on, let's go!" said Danny again, but the three of them only stood there, all together, unharmed. Langley looked at his brothers, both of them, and smiled. He sighed a deep, contented sigh. They were about to head down the hill.

"Let's go," said Langley.

"Do you want to leave?" said Delia.

"That's what Danny said. We all used to come up here with a wagon that we had. It had no sides and these steel wheels. It was an old thing, and we were small enough so that all three of us could fit on it together," said Langley.

"Brian used to steer, and we would start right up here and by the time we reached the bottom we were going like mad."

They looked down the hill. Leonard's Hill was steep and straight. Langley remembered that it used to have elm trees arching overhead, but those were all gone now. There were no houses on Leonard's Hill, and there was barely any traffic. But the road looked like it hadn't been paved since he was a kid. It was cracked and bulging with frost heaves. *There's no way you could drive a wagon down that pavement today,* thought Langley.

"I haven't been here for years. I used to even avoid it when I was on the beat, driving around town," he said

"Can you hear Danny's voice?"

"I can hear his voice, his voice when he was happy, not lying on the ground, you know?" He could almost feel the speed of flying down the hill. He closed his eyes and heard the three of them laughing and shouting.

"Let's go," he heard Danny say as they pushed the wagon with their feet to get their momentum going. "Let's go!" Langley was gently nodding his head in assent.

"Let's walk to the bottom of the hill," said Delia. She grabbed his arm, and they walked down together. When Langley looked down at the pavement it was as though he knew every inch of that road. He had seen it speeding by just inches below his feet hundreds of times.

"I always wondered if my parents knew what we were doing here," said Langley. "I think if they had ever found out, they would have stopped it." He smiled at the thought.

"They knew," said Delia.

"You think so?"

"Of course they did. They wanted their boys to live in the world."

"I suppose so."

"You had fun here," said Delia.

"Oh, God, just the three of us, over and over and over again."

Fifty-Two

December 20. Antonio and Langley walked down along the stone wall, and they stepped over the wall and onto the landfill.

It was an overcast day, and snowflakes drifted through the air. They didn't really fall. A few weightless flakes simply swirled in the air. There was a gentle winter blow, and in the air they could smell the familiar aromas of winter and wood smoke from fires a long way off, and they could hear snatches of voices, children's voices.

Antonio walked out to the middle of the landfill, which had stopped operating weeks ago. The earth movers had stopped in their tracks; they were sitting there rusting. The breeze blew concrete dust across the surface of the land. Langley had the feeling they were walking on the moon. It was so quiet it seemed as though no one had ever been there.

"You know, when I walk around my land sometimes it makes me wonder why I never married," said Antonio. "Then again, if I had married I wouldn't be able to do what I'm about to do."

Langley didn't know what he meant by that, but he didn't say anything. Antonio squinted as he looked off into the distance. They looked out at the dust snaking along in front of them. From this perch they could see all the way to the White Mountains. The air was so clear they could see their snowy tops.

Antonio crouched down and picked up some pieces of gravel and shook the tiny concrete bits in his hand like a pair of dice. Everything around them was gray and white. He threw the stones onto the ground and looked around the site. He stood.

"Well," he said. He shook his head and kept looking off into the distance.

The sky was winter quiet. The trees far down below them formed a sea of tangled gray branches, and Langley still marveled at how the land laid itself bare in the winter.

They could see all of Fenton from this perspective, the houses and buildings and streets and roads, the cars moving slowly toward their destinations, and the trails of smoke coming from chimneys throughout the town. He could see the Oquossoc, which looked sluggish and black as though its current had slowed almost to a stop. Lights were coming on inside houses for as far as they could see.

Christmas lights twinkled all over town. They were microscopic dots in the distance, no bigger than the farthest star in the universe, their light no brighter than that. The Fenton landscape was punctuated by thousands and thousands of blue, red, white, green, orange and yellow lights, spread out as far as they could see. The evening air made their light flutter gently.

Langley wondered what his kids were doing. He had mailed them their presents earlier that day.

Down to the west was the finished Dirty Books store building, sitting empty. It was a tiny block of concrete, barely noticeable in the distance.

Antonio said he wanted to get off this barren terrain. They walked past the spot where they had first seen the eagle. "I don't like it when things die," Antonio said. "It makes me sad."

Antonio had been very careful to let the wild creatures around him live their own lives. He had huge wasp nests hanging from his apple trees every summer, but he let them alone, and the wasps never bothered him. He let the garden snakes roam, and the deer and the fireflies and the dragonflies could do what they wanted to do. The bats that flew out of his barn every night had free reign, because Antonio knew that these creatures were here before him. "The animals will outlast me," he'd say.

The only things Antonio said he killed gleefully were mosquitoes and ticks, but he knew he was forgiven for that. He said he wanted most things to live the kind of life he had been able to live, unbothered, unprovoked, to live his life out in its natural rhythms and to last its natural appointed time.

They came down off the hill and stopped in Antonio's back yard. It had grown dark and cold. Antonio took two feathers out of his jacket pocket. Langley realized they were the two feathers Antonio had plucked from the solitary crowned eagle all those months ago. Antonio stuck them into the cracks of an old fence post, and they fluttered in the wind. The barbs of the feathers had cracked. The feathers looked old and beat and fragile.

"Let's go into the house," said Antonio. Inside Antonio fixed himself a black and tan. He had one every day. He handed Langley a pint glass full of Harp. "It'll be Christmas in a couple of days," he said in a kind of distant, offhanded way. "Do you still celebrate the holiday?"

"No, I haven't done anything since the kids moved away," Langley said. "It doesn't mean anything to me. Maybe this year, with Delia."

"I don't either," said Antonio. His mind seemed far away, which disconcerted Langley. Antonio was usually so focused. "I used to go up to the back and cut down a tree and decorate it with some ornaments. I haven't done that in, I don't know, years and years."

He put down his glass. "I have something for you." He went into another room and came back with a framed photo and a small box. "This is a picture taken of me at Fort Devens, just before I was shipped overseas," he said. "This is November 1950."

He looked at the photo. He stared into it. He didn't hand it over to Langley right away. "I hated being in that goddamn war," Antonio said, "but this is a good picture of me." He handed it to Langley, and Langley looked at the handsome young man in black and white.

Antonio was smiling in the picture, but the photo looked cropped. It looked like Antonio had his arm around someone, and Langley could see the edge of what looked like a skirt or a dress just at the edge of the photo. Langley didn't ask Antonio about it. He didn't want to embarrass the old man.

"It's a great picture of you," said Langley.

"That's for both you and Delia," he said.

"Thank you." Antonio handed Langley the small box. Langley opened it and saw Antonio's Bronze Star. "Oh, I can't take this," Langley said.

"Sure you can," Antonio said. He sat down on the stool in his kitchen and handed Langley a card. "Open that."

"Antonio, really, I ..."

"Open the card."

Inside the envelope inside was an engraved card. It looked like a fancy wedding invitation, and it read, "For bravery in the face of enemy pine trees."

Langley looked at the card and looked at Antonio. "You knew why I was so nervous."

"I ran into your father one day at the bank. I told him about you, and he told me about you."

"Huh," said Langley, "but your Bronze Star, Antonio."

"Listen." Antonio drew in a deep breath. "So much of what I have, or had, I was going to give to my children if I had had any, but …" Here Antonio shook his head almost imperceptibly, but it was a gesture weighted with sadness and regret nonetheless. "Obviously, that didn't work out. So now I find myself giving things away to people who should have them."

"OK," was all Langley could say. He was looking down at the Bronze Star because he was afraid that if he looked Antonio in the eyes, Antonio would see how sad he was for the old man. The medal was polished, and the ribbon looked fresh, as though the award had never been taken out of the box.

"I made a decision a little while ago that I want you to know about," Antonio said. Langley put down the picture and the box. "I've set aside this land, my house and the land here, so that it can't be developed. I've made it a conservation easement, just like the parcel next door. It's protected from anyone buying it, selling it, or putting anything up on it. I've set up a trust to keep the house and property in order, which I've put you and Delia in charge of. You're the trustees. You can live here with your children. But you and your children and their children have to make sure no one does anything to this land. You can let it go completely to seed, for all I care, but it can't be developed."

Langley took in a deep breath. He was both overwhelmed and grateful. It didn't seem as though there was any way to accept such a huge gesture gracefully. If someone had asked how he would have wanted everything to turn out, Langley would have said he would want to live in Antonio's house with Delia and take care of it and let the wildlife live just as Antonio had.

So he didn't know what to say. He stood there with his hands at his sides, just looking down at the floor. But then he lifted his head, and the two men just nodded to each other.

"When I die, I'm going to be cremated. You'll take my ashes and put them in a hole you've dug, and then plant a little tree right in the hole, and you can watch that grow," said Antonio. "If I die in the winter, you'll just have to hold on to me until it's spring."

"I promise," said Langley.

"Plant a nice tree," said Antonio, and all Langley did was put his hand on Antonio's shoulder and squeeze it in such a way so that the old man knew Langley loved him.

"I also don't want you to do anything cute and go naming the land here," said Antonio. "I don't want it to be called Eagle Pass or anything cute."

Langley nodded. He knew by his tone and his expression that Antonio was completely serious.

"Just take care of the place," Antonio said.

Fifty-Three

When the time came years later, Langley planted a hickory tree, which Antonio would have scoffed at if Langley had ever told him. But Langley knew that Antonio wouldn't have minded. He and Delia dug a hole and poured in Antonio's ashes and planted the tree.

Almost from the day he was born, Langley and Delia took their little boy, Jesse James Calhoun, outside to enjoy this little sanctuary in Fenton. They let him sit in the fields and in the dirt in the garden that Delia tended.

"He's going to be a pirate," said Delia of their little boy, "just like his dad."

When he was first able, Jesse would walk through the wooded areas of the property and sit on a rock and watch the wildlife crawl and slink by. He would catch insects and hold them triumphantly over his head. He would let the newts sit in the palm of his hand, and he'd cup small frogs and try to stop them from hopping back out to the ground.

Jesse James danced along with the dragonflies while Langley mowed the lawn and as Delia checked her tomato plants for worms and blight. He chased their chickens and fed them slugs.

One day during their fourth summer, as they walked around the land, all three of them holding hands with their little boy in the middle, they saw a beautiful big bird fly overhead. It swooped down, gliding on the wind. They all watched the bird in its nice, even flight. They shielded their eyes from the summer sun.

"Oh, my God," said Delia, "that's a Golden Eagle." She looked at Langley and smiled.

Langley watched the bird circle in the sky. Then he and Delia went back to work in the summer sun. Langley felled a big ash that they would later cut up for firewood. Delia checked the cucumbers, which looked robust, and the acorn squash, which were dying on the vine, and she looked at the snap peas as they worked their way up the fence surrounding the garden.

Their little son toddled across the grass. Langley looked at Delia as she weeded the garden. He looked at her face, her lithe body, and her beautiful hands as she snatched at the unruly grass.

"Hey, Jesse," Langley called out as their son seemed to be moving too far away. Delia looked up. Jesse turned to face his father. His swift pivot made him a little unsteady, and he dropped right on his bottom. Langley picked Jesse up and brought him over to Delia.

They were in the garden. They had spread some old pieces of carpet in one corner not only to kill the grass underneath so they could expand the garden next year, but also to give the snakes a cool place to rest underneath in the hot summer sun.

With Jesse at his side, Langley leaned over the carpet and quickly lifted up a corner of the old floor covering. A small garter snake was coiled up in the dry dirt. By the time it realized it was exposed and tried to squirm away, Langley had grabbed it and handed it to Jesse.

"Be careful," said Langley to the boy. "Don't squeeze." The snake craned its long neck and arched around and snapped at Jesse's fingers. Jesse opened his hands, and the snake wriggled away and disappeared through the garden fence. Delia and Langley looked at each other and smiled. Jesse laughed, and as he did, they heard the call of the eagle. The bird was sitting high above them.

Delia looked at Langley. She went over to him, and they both picked up their son. It seemed as though the whole world was bathed in sunlight. Jesse looked up at the bird and pointed at it. The eagle sat bobbing on the end of a branch at the top of Antonio's old bull pine. It was the one Antonio tried to kill but didn't die. The eagle flapped its gorgeous wings.

"Oh, he sees us," said Delia.

The bird stared back. He leaned forward, his head darting around, looking in each direction. He was proudly keeping a fierce eye of protection over everything that was happening below.

"Langley," Delia said, her voice echoing through the trees.

Langley smiled. He closed his eyes and lifted his face to the sun. He felt protected by Delia and held aloft by Jesse. He was sustained by the memory of Antonio, and he knew that Danny and Brian were always going to straggle along beside him with their goofy smiles and raggedy clothes.

"Let's go," Langley heard Danny whisper in his ear.

And so Langley walked into the sun with his family. He knew that all of them—all of them—were loved, and all of them were safe.

Meet Author Lars R. Trodson

Lars Trodson was born and raised in Rhode Island. From as early as he can remember, he wanted to be a writer. He started at his high school paper at Providence Country Day School and worked as a daily newspaper reporter and editor in New England for more than twenty years after college.

Lars is the recipient of numerous industry awards for his column writing and reporting. He is a published essayist and poet, and he co-founded the popular blog www.roundtablepictures.com in 2007.

He currently lives in New Hampshire. *Eagles Fly Alone* is his first novel.

CPSIA information can be obtained at www.ICGtesting.com
Printed in the USA
LVOW070325150911

246383LV00001B/13/P